Sex Slaves of the Dragon Tong

A Yellow Peril Triptych

By

F. Paul Wilson

SEX SLAVES OF THE DRAGON TONG

First edition 2012

CONTENTS

Foreword

Foreword

Yellow Peril…how can a phrase that reeks so of racism and paranoia yield a body of fiction so…cool?

The term originated in the late nineteenth century. Chinese immigrants were flooding our western shore and spreading throughout the country at a time when their homeland was growing more and more militaristic. Could this mass immigration be a silent first wave of an eventual invasion?

Chinese villains became regulars in the penny dreadfuls. In 1913 Sax Rohmer created the paradigm for all oriental evil from then on: Fu-Manchu. (He dropped the hyphen after the third novel.) I became enthralled with the good doctor at age fifteen when I met him in the pages of the Pyramid reprint of *The Insidious Doctor Fu Manchu*. I became a fan of the pulps and particularly enjoyed the exotic yellow-peril stories they regularly featured. (Even the Shadow had a recurring nemesis named Shiwan Khan.)

So when Joe Lansdale asked me to contribute to an anthology called *Retro Pulp Tales*, I said it had to be Yellow Peril. I decided it would involve a face-off between two fictional titans of the times. I came up with the most lurid title I could think of and, after that, the story pretty damn near wanted to write itself.

But since I was going to set it in the 1930s, I first wanted to get a feel for the times. So I found a collection of Yellow Peril stories (*It's Raining Corpses in Chinatown*, edited by Don Hutchison) and read half a dozen. The casual racism surprised me. The operative word here is "casual." I detected no hate in the true sense of the word; more like workaday denigration of another race.

In polite conversation they were called Chinamen or Orientals (not "Asian," as political correctness now dictates). But down on the street they were chinks and coolies. Chinatown was No-Tickee-No-Shirty-ville. As I said, casual, accepted. Like those 1930s scenes in *Something the Lord Made* (the film about the brilliant Vivien Thomas) where the black folks step off the path and tip their hats as the white folks pass as if it's the most natural thing in the world. Racism, pure and simple, but taken for granted by both sides. Like when I was a kid and loved Little Richard's music. It was known as "race music" on the radio, but called "nigger music" at backyard barbecues – and no one raised even an eyebrow.

My how things have changed.

But the stories in the following triptych don't take place in modern-day America. You'll hear cops and detectives refer to their fellow citizens of Chinese descent just the way they did in the 1930s. That has upset readers in the past, but to do less is to betray the setting, the characters, and the genre. This is the way it was. We shouldn't forget that, shouldn't sweep it under the rug and pretend it never existed. If nothing else, we can be grateful this is no longer the way it is.

F. Paul Wilson
The Jersey Shore
2012

Sex Slaves of the Dragon Tong

"You'll find my Margot, won't you?" Mr. Kachmar said. "Please?"

Detective Third Grade Brad Brannigan felt the weight of the portly man's imploring gaze as Chief Hanrahan ushered him out of his office.

"Of course he will," the Chief told him. "He's one of our best men."

Brannigan smiled and nodded with a confidence as false as the Chief's words. He was baffled as to why he, the greenest detective in the San Francisco PD, had been called in on this of all cases.

Mr. Kachmar turned at the door. "I hope you don't mind, but I've hired a private detective as well. I can't leave any stone unturned. You understand, I hope."

Brannigan understood, but he could tell the Chief didn't like it one bit.

When the door finally closed, sealing out Mr. Kachmar, the Chief turned and exhaled through puffed cheeks.

"Lord preserve us from friends of the mayor with wayward daughters, aye, Brannigan?"

As Hanrahan dropped into the creaking chair behind his desk, Brannigan searched for a response.

"I appreciate the compliment, Chief, but we both know I'm not one of your best men."

The Chief smiled. "That we do, lad. That we do."

"Then why–?"

"Because I'll be knowing about Margot Kachmar and she's a bit of a hellion. Twenty years old and not a thought in her head about anyone but herself. Probably found a fellow she sparked to and went off with him on a lark. Wouldn't be the first time."

"But her father looked so worried."

"I'd be worried too if I had a daughter like that. Kachmar has only himself to blame. Rich folks like him give their kids too long a leash. Make it tough for the rest of us. You should hear my own daughter." He mimicked a young woman's voice. "'This isn't the dark ages, Daddy. It's nineteen thirty-eight.'" He huffed and returned to his normal tone. "I wouldn't care if it was nineteen *fifty*-eight, you've got to be after watching your daughters every single minute. Watching 'em like a hawk."

While trying his best to look interested in the chief's domestic philosophy, Brannigan cut in as soon as he had a chance.

"What do I do about the private dick he hired?"

The Chief made a dismissive gesture. "Freeze him out. We don't need no hired gumshoes muddying the waters."

"Okay. Will do. Now to the girl: Where was she last seen?"

"Washington and Grant."

"Chinatown?"

"At least that's what her girlfriend says." Hanrahan winked. "Covering for her, I'll bet. You give that one a bit of hard questioning and she'll be coming around."

"But Chinatown is…"

"Yes, Sorenson's beat. But I can't very well be asking him to look into it, can I."

Of course he couldn't. Sorenson was laid up in the hospital with some strange malady.

"And," Chief Hanrahan added, "I can't very well be pulling my best men off other cases and sending them to No-tickee-no-shirtee-ville to question a bunch of coolies about some young doxy who'll show up on her own in a day or two. So you're getting the nod, Detective Brannigan."

Brad felt heat in his cheeks and knew they were reddening. For a fair-skinned redhead like him, a blush was always waiting in the wings, ready to prance onstage at an instant's notice.

The chief's meaning was clear: I don't want to waste someone useful, so you take it.

Brad repressed a dismayed sigh. He knew this was because of the Jenkins case. Missing a vital clue had left him looking like an amateur. As a result the rest of the detectives at the station had had weeks of fun at his expense. But though the razzing was over, Chief Hanrahan still hadn't assigned him to anything meaty. Brannigan wound up with the leftovers. If he didn't get some arrests to his credit he'd never make second grade.

Stop feeling sorry for yourself, he thought. Your day will come. It just won't be today.

*

A bulldog of a man in a baggy suit was waiting in the hall. He handed Brannigan a card that identified him as an operative with a local detective agency.

"Kachmar hired me," he said.

"So I heard."

"How come Sorenson's not working this?"

Brannigan hid his resentment at the question. "He's sick."

"Yeah? Too bad. What's your first stop?"

Brannigan figured he'd follow the chief's suggestion.

"The friend."

"Okay. I'm heading for Chink City. We can meet up there."

"Yeah, maybe."

"Listen. No need to get territorial on this. We both want to find her. We can get this settled and save each other time."

Brannigan figured he could use all the help he could get, but didn't want credit going to some dick for hire.

"Okay."

The detective started to turn away, then swung back. "Say, you ever hear of the Lord of Strange Deaths?"

Sounded like something out of one of those pulp magazines that littered the newsstands. Brannigan told him the truth. "No. Who's that?"

"A chink I've been hunting for years. You hear him that mentioned down there, you let me know, okay?"

"What's this got to do with Margot Kachmar?"

He winked. "Side project." Then he walked off.

*

Brannigan tracked Margot's friend Katy Webber to her parents' home, a stone mansion in Pacific Heights.

Five minutes with her were all it took to convince him that she wasn't covering for Margot. She was too upset.

"One moment she was with me," she said through her tears, "and the next minute she wasn't! I turned to look in a jewelry store window – that was why we went there, to look for some jade – and when I turned back to point out a necklace, she was gone!"

"And you didn't see anyone suspicious hanging about? No one following you?"

"Not that I noticed. And Margot never mentioned seeing anyone. The streets were crowded with people and cars and…I don't understand how she could have disappeared like that."

Neither did Brannigan. "You must have seen *something*."

"Well…"

"What?"

"It might be nothing, but I saw this black car pulling away and I thought…" She shook her head. "I thought I saw the back of a blond head through the rear window."

"Margot's head?"

Katy shrugged and looked miserable. "I don't know. It was just a glimpse and then the car turned the corner."

"Do you remember the license plate? The make? The model?"

Katy responded to each question with a shake of her head. "I don't know cars. I did notice that it had four doors, but beyond that…"

Swell, Brannigan thought. A black sedan. San Francisco had thousands and thousands of them.

But Katy's story convinced him that someone had kidnapped Margot Kachmar. In broad daylight to boot. He'd start where she was last seen, at Washington and Grant, and move out from there.

But he'd move on his own. This was his chance to get himself out of Dutch with the chief, so he'd keep it to himself for now. If Hanrahan got wind that this was a real kidnapping, he'd pull Brannigan and put someone else on it sure.

Someone in that area of Chinatown had to remember something. All he needed to do was ask the right person. And that meant his next step was good old-fashioned door-to-door detective work.

*

"Wah!" Yu Chaoyang cried. "Slow the car!"

Jiang Zhifu looked around, startled. He and Yu occupied the back of one of the black Packard sedans owned by Yan Yuap Tong. An underling Yu had brought from Singapore sat behind the wheel. All three wore identical black cotton outfits with high collars and frog-buttoned fronts, although Yu's large girth required twice as much fabric as Jiang's; each jacket was embroidered with a golden dragon over the left breast; each man wore his hair woven into a braid that dangled from beneath a traditional black skullcap.

"What is wrong?" Jiang said as the car slowed almost to a stop.

"Nothing is wrong, my tong brother. In fact, something is very right." A chubby finger pointed toward the sidewalk. "Look and marvel."

Jiang peered through the side window glass and saw a typical Chinatown scene: pushcarts laden with fruits and vegetables, fish live and dead, fluttering caged birds and roasted ducks; weaving among them was the usual throng of shoppers, a mix of locals and tourists.

Yu had come to America just last month on a mission for his father, head of the Yan Yuap Tong's house in Singapore; Jiang had volunteered to guide him through the odd ways of this strange country.

Yu was proving to be a trial. Arrogant and headstrong, he did not give proper face to his tong brothers here in San Francisco. Some of that might be anticipated from the son of a tong chief from home, but Yu went beyond proper bounds. No one expected him to kowtow, but he should show more respect.

"I don't understand," Jiang said.

Yu turned to face him. He ran a long sinuous tongue over his lips, brushing his thin drooping mustache in the process. His smile narrowed further his puffy lids until they were mere slits through which his onyx eyes gleamed.

"Red hair! Red hair!"

Jiang looked again and saw a little girl, no more than ten years old, standing by a cart, looking at a cage full of sparrows. She wore a red dress with white trim, but her unruly hair was even redder: a bushy flame, flaring around her face like the corona of an eclipse.

"Look at her." Yu's voice became a serpent, slithering through the car. "What a price I can fetch for her!"

"But she's a child."

"Yes! Precisely! I have a buyer in Singapore who specializes in children, and a red-haired child...aieee! He will pay anything for her!"

Jiang's stomach tightened. A child...

"Are you forgetting the conditions set by the Mandarin?"

"May maggots eat the eyes of your Mandarin!"

Jiang couldn't help a quick look around. He thanked his ancestors that the windows were closed. Someone might have heard.

"Do not speak of him so! And do not even think of breaking your agreement with him!"

Yu leaned closer. "Where do your loyalties lie, Jiang? With your tong, or with this mysterious Mandarin you all kowtow to?"

"I am loyal to Yan Yuap, but I am also fond of my skin. And if you wish to keep yours, you will heed my warning. Those who oppose his will wind up dead or are never seen again."

"Eh-yeh!" Yu waved a dismissive hand. "By tomorrow night I will be at sea with this barbarous country far behind me."

"Yes. You will be gone, but I will still have to live here."

Yu grinned, showing mottled teeth, stained from his opium pipe. "That is not my worry."

"Do not be so sure. The Mandarin's reach is long. He has never been known to break his word, and he has no mercy toward those who break theirs to him. I beg you not to do this."

The grin turned into a sneer. "America has softened you, Jiang. You shake like a frightened old woman."

Jiang looked away. This man was a fool. Yu had come to America for women – white women he could sell to the Singapore brothels. The lower level houses there and the streets around them were full of dolla-dolla girls shipped in from the farmlands. But the upper echelon salons that provided gambling as well as sex needed something special to bring in the high rollers. White women were one such draw. And *blond* white women were the ultimate lure.

Since nothing in San Francisco's Chinese underworld happened without the Mandarin's consent – or without his receiving a share of the proceeds – Yu had needed prior approval of his plan. How he had raged at the ignominy of such an arrangement, but he had been persuaded that he would have no success without it.

The Mandarin had set two conditions. First: take only one woman from San Francisco, all the rest from surrounding cities and towns. The second: no children. He did not care to weather a Lindbergh-style investigation.

Jiang said, "We took a girl here only yesterday, and now a child from these same streets. You will be breaking both conditions with this act."

Yu smiled. "No, Jiang. *We* will be breaking them. We will watch and wait, and when the time is right, you will pluck this delicious little berry from her branch."

Jiang agonized as Yu had the driver circle the block again and again. Yes, he was a member of the Yan Yuap Tong, but he was also a member of a more powerful and far-flung society. And the Mandarin was one of its leaders. Jiang was the Mandarin's eyes within the Yan Yuap Tong, and as such he would have to report this. Not that he would mind the slightest seeing the worst happen to Yu, but he prayed to his ancestors that the Mandarin wouldn't make him pay too for his part in the transgression.

"Wah!" Yu said. "She has turned the corner. There is no one about! Now! Now!"

Fumes filled the car as Jiang poured chloroform onto a rag. He jumped out, the soft slap of his slippers on the pavement the only sign of his presence; he clamped the rag over the child's face and was dragging her back toward the car's open door when a ball of light brown fur darted across the sidewalk toward them. Jiang heard a growl of fury, saw bared fangs, and then the thing was upon him, tearing at the flesh of his arm.

He cried out for help and received it in the report of a pistol. The dog yelped and tumbled backward to lie twitching on the sidewalk. The child's wild struggles – she was a tough little one – slowed and ceased as the chloroform did its work. Jiang shoved her into the back seat between Yu and himself. The car lurched into motion. Jiang glanced back and saw a pool of blood forming around the head of the sandy-haired dog.

He looked at the now unconscious child and saw Yu caressing one of her pale, bare thighs.

"Ah, my little quail," he cooed, "I would so like to use the trip home to teach you the thousand ways to please a man, but alas you must remain a virgin if I am to take full profit from you."

Jiang closed his eyes and trembled inside. He had to tell the Mandarin of this. He prayed he'd survive the meeting.

*

"I've run into a blank wall," Brannigan said.

"And so you've come to me for help."

Looking at Detective Sergeant Hank Sorenson now, Brannigan wished he'd gone elsewhere.

He'd had a nodding acquaintance with Sorenson at the station, but the figure pressed between the sheets in the hospital bed before him was a caricature of the man Brannigan had known.

He tried not to stare at the sunken cheeks, the glassy, feverish eyes, the sallow, sweaty skin as pale as his hospital gown. The slow smile that stretched Sorenson's lips and bared his teeth was ghastly.

"You mean to tell me you walked up to Chinatown residents and asked them what they saw?"

The whole afternoon had been a frustrating progression of singsong syllables, expressionless yellow faces with gleaming slanted eyes that told him nothing.

"I didn't see that I had any other option."

"You can't treat chinks like regular people, Brad. You can't ask them a direct question. They're devious, crafty, always circling."

Brannigan bristled at Sorenson's attitude, like a teacher chiding a student for not knowing his lesson.

"Well, be that as it may, no one saw anything."

Sorenson barked a phlegmy laugh. "Oh, they saw all right. They're just not going to tell an outsider. Not if they know what's good for them."

"What's that mean?"

"The Mandarin. You do not cross the Mandarin."

Sorenson went on to explain about Chinatown's lord of crime. Then added, "If this Kachmar girl is a blond, you might be dealing with a white slave ring. The Yan Yuap Tong – also called the Dragon Tong because their symbol is a dragon – has been involved in that before. The tongsters probably have your missing girl's photo on its way back to Singapore already, to get the bidding started."

Brannigan had heard of Oriental rings that abducted white women for sex slaves, but he'd never expected that Margot Kachmar–

"Check Oakland and Marin and maybe San Jose," Sorenson was saying. "See if they've had a blonde or two gone missing recently."

"Why there?"

"Because police departments don't communicate nearly enough. Someday they will, but with things as they are, spreading out the abductions lessens the chances of anyone spotting a pattern."

Oakland…San Jose…that seemed like a lot of legwork with slim chance of a turning up anything useful.

"Why don't I go straight to the source? This Mandarin character…where do I find him?"

Sorenson began to shake with ague. His head fell back on the pillow. When the tremors eased…

"No one knows. He hides his identity even from his fellow Chinese. Just as well – you don't want to find him. I came close and look what it got me."

"I don't understand."

"I was homing in on the Mandarin's identity, getting closer than anyone before me, and then, a week ago, something got into my house and bit me."

"Something?"

"A giant millipede, bright red, at least eight inches long, crawled into my bed and bit me on the shoulder. I managed to smash it with a shoe as it raced away, but only got the back half. The front half broke off and escaped. Bug scientists over at the university says it only exists in Borneo."

"But what's that got to do–?"

"It was *put* in my house, you idiot!" Sorenson snapped, a faint tinge of color seeping into his cheeks. "By one of the Mandarin's men. And look what it's done to me!"

He pulled the hospital gown off his left shoulder to reveal a damp dressing. He ripped that off.

"It's due for a change anyway. Have a look."

Brannigan saw an ulcerated crater perhaps two inches across penetrating deep into the flesh of Sorenson's shoulder. Its base was red and bloody. A quick look was more than enough for Brannigan, but as he was turning away he thought he saw something move within the bloody fluid. He looked again–

And jumped back.

Many little things were moving in the base of the ulcer.

"What–?"

Sorenson's expression was bleak. Brannigan could see he was trying to keep up a brave face.

"Yeah. The bug didn't poison me. I wish it had. Instead it laid a bunch of eggs in me, a thousand, maybe a million of them. And they keep hatching. I think they're getting into my system, eating me alive from the inside."

"Can't the doctors stop it?"

He shook his head. "They've never seen anything like–"

He clasped a hand over his mouth as he broke off into a fit of coughing. The harsh barks seemed to be coming from somewhere around his ankles. With a final wet hack he stopped.

A look of horror twisted his features as he stared at his palm. It was filled with bloody phlegm, and Brannigan could swear he saw something wriggling within the glob, something with many, many legs.

"Oh, God!" Sorenson wailed, his composure finally broken. "Call the doctor! Get the nurse in here! Hurry!"

Brannigan turned and ran for the hallway. Behind him he heard the wrenching sound of a grown man sobbing.

*

Jiang could not keep his body from shaking as he knelt with his forehead pressed against the cold stone floor. The Mandarin stood over him, eerily silent. Jiang had told him what had transpired on the street. It had been hours ago, but he had come as soon as he could get away.

At last the master spoke, his voice soft, the tone sibilant.

"So…Yu Chaoyang has disobeyed me and endangered all we have worked for here. I half expected this from such a man. The Japanese are overrunning our China, slaughtering its people, and Yu thinks only of adding to his already swollen coffers."

"Venerable, I tried to dissuade him but–"

"I am sure you did your best, Jiang Zhifu, but apparently it wasn't enough."

No-no-no! cried a terrified voice within Jiang. Let him not be angry!

But Jiang's outer voice was wise enough to remain silent.

"However," the master said, "I will allow you to redeem yourself."

"Oh, Illustrious! This miserable offspring of a worm is endlessly grateful."

"Rise."

Jiang eased to his feet and stood facing the Master, but looked at him only from the corner of his eye. The man known throughout Chinatown as the Mandarin – even Jiang did not know his true name – was tall, lean, high-shouldered, standing bamboo straight with his hands folded inside his sleeves of his flowing turquoise robe; his hair was thin and covered with a brimless cap beaded with coral. He had a high, domed forehead and thin lips, but his eyes – light green, their color intensified by the shade of his robe – were unlike any Jiang had ever seen.

"Where is the child now?"

"Yu has her in the tonghouse, but soon he will head for his ship and set sail. Shall I stop him? Shall I see to it that he suffers the same fate as that too-curious detective?"

The master shook his head. "No. Did the child see you?"

"No, Magnificent. I took her from behind and she was soon unconscious."

"Then she cannot point a finger of blame at a Chinaman. Good. You will return to the tonghouse and light a red lamp in the room where the child is kept. I will send a few of my dacoits to see that she is returned to the streets. You must be present so that no suspicion falls on you. Then let Yu go to his ship and set sail with the rest of his cargo. He will never see home. He – Jiang, you are bleeding."

"It is nothing, Eminent. The child's dog bit me as I pulled her into the car. It is nothing."

"The red-haired little girl had a dog, you say? What kind of dog?"

"A scruffy mongrel. May this unworthy snail ask why such an Esteemed One as you would ask?"

When the master did not answer, Jiang dared a glance at his face and saw the unimaginable: a look of uncertainty in those green eyes.

"Exalted…did this miserable slug say something wrong?"

"No, Jiang. I had a thought, that is all… about a certain little red-haired girl who must not be touched…ever." He turned and stepped to the single high small window in the north wall of the tiny room. "It could not possibly be she, but if it is…and if she is harmed…all the ancestors of all the members of the Yan Yuap Tong will not save it from doom…a doom that could spread to us as well."

*

Brannigan leaned against the center railing of the hospital's front steps and sucked deep draughts of the foggy night air.

Sorenson…a tough, no-nonsense cop… reduced to a weeping child. It gave him a bad case of the willies. Who was this Mandarin? And more important, was he involved in Margot Kachmar's disappearance?

Feeling steadier, Brannigan stepped down to the sidewalk and headed for his car radio car. He needed to call in. A catchy song by Frances Day, "I've Got You Under My Skin," echoed unwelcomed in his head. From somewhere in the fog a newsboy called out the headlines of the evening edition. As he passed a silver Rolls Royce its rear door opened and an accented voice spoke from the dark interior.

"Please step inside. Someone wishes to speak to you."

Someone? That could very well be the Mandarin. Well, Brannigan damn well wanted to speak to him too, but on his terms, not in the back of a mysterious limousine.

He backed away. "Have him meet me down at the station," he said, backing away. "We'll have a nice long chat there."

Brannigan jumped at the sound of another voice close behind him, almost in his ear.

"He would speak to you now. Into the car please."

Brannigan reached for his pistol but his shoulder holster was empty. He whirled and found himself face to face with a gaunt Chinaman dressed in a black business suit, a white shirt, and a black tie. A black fedora finished off the look. His expression was bland, his tone matter of fact, but his features had a sinister, almost cruel cast.

He held up Brannigan's .38 between them but did not point it at him. He gestured to the car with his free hand.

"Please."

Brannigan's first instinct was to run, but figured all he'd gain by that was a slug in the back. Probably better than a millipede in his bed, but he decided on the car option. Maybe he'd find an opening along the way to make a break.

With his bladder clenching, he ducked inside. The door slammed behind him, drenching him in darkness. He could sense but not see whoever was seated across from him. As the car began moving – the thin chink was also the driver, it seemed – Brannigan leaned forward, straining to see his host.

"Are you…?" His mouth was dry so he wet his lips. "Are you the Mandarin?"

A soft laugh. "Oh, no. I would not serve that one."

"Then why do you want to speak to me?"

"It is not I, Detective Brannigan. It is another. Hush now and save your words for him."

The glare from a passing streetlight illuminated the interior for a second, leaving Brannigan in a state of shock. The other occupant was a turbaned giant who looked as if he'd just stepped out of Arabian nights.

The car turned west on California, taking them away from Chinatown. A few minutes later they stopped at a side entrance to the Fairmont Hotel, perched atop Nob Hill like a granite crown. The driver and the giant escorted Brannigan by to an elevator in an empty service hallway. Inside the car, the driver inserted a key into the control panel and up they went.

After a swift, stomach-sinking ride, the elevator doors opened into a huge suite, richly furnished and decorated with palm trees and ornate marble columns reaching to its high, glass-paned ceiling.

An older man rose from a sofa. He was completely bald with pale gray eyes. He wore black tuxedo pants and a white dress shirt ornamented with a huge diamond stickpin. Brannigan spotted a black dress jacket and tie draped over a nearby chair. A long thick cigar smoldered in his left hand; he extended the right as he strode forward.

"Detective Brannigan, I presume. Thank you for coming."

Brannigan, flabbergasted, shook the man's hand. This wasn't at all what he'd expected.

"I didn't have much choice."

He eyed his two escorts as they took up positions behind his host. The driver had removed his hat, revealing a bald dome; glossy black hair fringed the sides and back of his scalp.

"Oh, I hope they didn't threaten you."

Brannigan was about to crack wise when he realized that they hadn't threatened him at all. If anything they'd been overly polite.

He studied the bald man. Something familiar about him…

"I've seen you before."

The man shrugged. "Despite my best efforts, my face now and again winds up in the papers."

"Who are you?"

"Let's just say I'm someone who prefers to move in and out of large cities without advertising his presence. Otherwise my time would be consumed by a parade of local politicians with their hands out, and I'd never get any work done."

"What do you want with me?"

"You were in Chinatown today asking about a missing girl, Margot Kachmar."

The statement startled Brannigan at first, but then he glanced at the Oriental driver and realized he shouldn't be surprised.

"That's police business."

"And now it's *my* business." A sudden, steely tone put a knife edge on the words. "My daughter was abducted from that same area this afternoon."

"She was? Did you tell the police?"

"That's what I'm doing now."

"I mean an official report and – never mind. Are you sure she was abducted?"

The bald man hooked a finger through the air and Brannigan followed him to the far side of a huge couch. Along the way he glanced out the tall windows and saw Russian Hill and San Francisco Bay stretching out below. This had to be the penthouse suite.

The man pointed to a sandy-furred mutt lying on a big red pillow. A thick bandage encircled its head.

"That's her dog. She goes nowhere without him. He was shot – luckily the bullet glanced off his skull instead of piercing it – and that can only mean that he was defending her. He almost died, but he's a tough one, just like his little owner."

Two in two days from the same neighborhood…this was not the pattern Sorenson had described.

"How old is your daughter, and is she blond?"

"She's a ten-year-old redhead – her hair's the same shade as yours."

Cripes. A kid. "Well, I'm sorry about what happened to her, but I don't think she's connected to the Kachmar girl. I–"

"What if I told you they were both dragged into a black Packard sedan? Most likely the same one?"

Katy Webber had described a black sedan. Maybe there was a connection after all.

The bald man said, "I have men out canvassing the neighborhoods right now, looking for that car."

"That's police business. You can't–"

"I can and I am. Don't worry – they'll be very discreet. But I'll make you a deal, detective: You share with me, I'll share with you. If I locate Miss Kachmar, I'll notify you. If you find my daughter alive and well I will see to it that you never have to worry about money for the rest of your life."

Brannigan felt a flush of anger. "I don't need to be bribed to do my job."

"It's not a bribe – it will be gratitude. Anything of mine you want you can have. I've made fortunes and lost them, gone from living in mansions to being penniless on the street and back to mansions. I'm good at making money. I can always replace my fortune. But I can't replace that little girl." The man seemed to lose his voice and Brannigan saw his throat work. When he recovered he added, "She means everything to me."

The nods from the turbaned giant and the driver said they felt the same. Brannigan was touched. He couldn't help it. And from the looks on all three faces he knew that if they were the first to discover the child's abductor, the mugg would never see trial.

He couldn't condone or allow the vigilantism he sensed brewing here. And for that reason he couldn't tell them what Sorenson had said about the Dragon Tong. He'd keep that to himself.

"I promise you that if I find her, you'll be the first to know."

The bald man put his hand out to the Chinese driver who placed Brannigan's pistol in it, then he fixed the detective with his pale gaze. "That is all I ask. Can my associates offer you a lift?"

"No thanks." He'd seen enough of the old man's chums for one evening. "I'll grab a cab."

He took the elevator down to the lobby level, but before going outside, he stopped at the front desk.

"Who's staying in the penthouse suite?" he asked the clerk. He flipped open his wallet, showing his shield. "And don't give me any malarkey about hotel policy."

The man hesitated, then shrugged. After consulting the guest register he shook his head.

"Sorry. It's unoccupied."

"Baloney! I was just up there."

Another shake of the head. "No occupant is listed. All I can tell you is this: The penthouse suite is on reserve – permanent reserve – but it doesn't say for whom."

Frustrated, Brannigan stormed from the hotel. He had more important things to do than argue with some hotel flunky.

*

Ten minutes later Brannigan was standing in the shadows across the street from the headquarters of the Dragon Tong. Its slanted cupola glistened with moisture from the fog. A few of the upper windows were lit, a pair of green-and-yellow paper lanterns hung outside the front entrance, but otherwise the angular building squatted dark and silent on its lot.

What now? Sorenson had told him how to find it, but now that he was here he couldn't simply walk in. Much as he hated to admit it, he was going to have to call Hanrahan for backup.

As he turned to go back to his radio car he noticed movement along the right flank of the tonghouse. Three monkey-like shadows were scaling the wall. He hurried across the street and crept closer to investigate. He found a rope hanging along the wall, disappearing into a third-story window lit by a red paper lantern.

Apparently someone else was interested in the tonghouse. He knew the three he'd seen shimmying up this rope were too small and agile to have been the bald guy and company.

He looked at the rope, tempted. This was one hell of a pickle. Go up or get help?

The decision was taken out of his hands when the rope snaked up the wall and out of reach. He cursed as he watched it disappear into the window.

But then he noticed a narrow door just to his right. He tried the handle – unlocked – and pushed it open. The slow creaks from the old hinges sounded like a cat being tortured. He cringed as he slipped into some sort of kitchen. He pulled his pistol and waited to see if anyone came to investigate.

When no one came, he slipped through the darkness, listening. The tonghouse seemed quiet. Most of the tongsters were probably home at this hour. But what of the thugs the tongs used as guards and enforcers? The chinks called them *boo hoo dow doy* – hatchet sons – and the newspapers called them "highbinders" because of the way they tied their braided queues up under their caps so no one could grab them if they needed to escape.

Did they go home too? Brannigan hoped so, but doubted it.

He stepped through a curtain into a small chamber lit by a single oil lamp, its walls bare except for a black lacquered door ornamented with gold dragons uncoiling from the corners. The door pulled outward and Brannigan found himself in an exotic, windowless room, empty except for a golden Buddha seated in a corner; a lamp and joss sticks smoked before it, their vapors wafting toward the high ceiling.

Something about the walls…he stepped closer and gasped as he ran his fingers over what he'd assumed to be wallpaper. But these peacock plumes weren't painted, they were the genuine article. And all four walls were lined with them.

Dazzled by its beauty, Brannigan stepped back to the center of the room and turned in a slow circle. No window, no door other than the one he'd come through. The room appeared to be a dead end.

But then he noticed the way the smoke from the joss sticks wavered on its path toward the ceiling. Air was flowing in from somewhere. He moved along the wall, inspecting the plumes until he found one with a wavering fringe. And another just below it. Air was filtering through a narrow crevice. He pushed at the wall on either side until he felt something give. He pushed harder and a section swung inward.

Ahead of Brannigan lay a long, dark, downsloping corridor, ending in a rectangle of wan, flickering light. The only sound was his own breathing.

He hesitated, then took a breath and started forward. He'd come this far…in for a dime, in for a dollar.

Pistol at ready, he crept down the passage as silently as his heavy regulation shoes would allow, pausing every few steps to listen. Nothing. All quiet.

When he reached the end he stopped. All he could see ahead was bare floor and wall, lit by a lamp in some unseen corner. Still hearing nothing, he risked a peek inside–

–and ducked back as he caught a flash of movement to his left. A black-handled hatchet whispered past the end of his nose and buried itself in the wall just inches to the right of his head.

And then a black-pajama-clad *boo hoo dow doy* with a high-cheeked, pockmarked face lunged at him with a raised dagger. His brutal features were contorted with rage as he shouted rapid-fire gibberish.

The report from Brannigan's pistol was deafening as it smashed a bullet through the chink's chest and sent him tumbling backward. Another black-clad tongster, a raw-boned, beady-eyed bugger, replaced him immediately, howling the same cry as he swung a hatchet at Brannigan's throat. He too fell with a bullet in his chest.

But then the doorway was filled with two more and then three, and more surging behind them. With only four rounds left in his revolver, Brannigan knew he had no chance of stopping this Mongol horde. He began backpedaling as the hatchetmen leaped over their fallen comrades and charged.

Brannigan fired as he retreated, making good use of his remaining rounds, slowing the black-clad gang's advance, but a small, primitive part of him began screeching in panic as it became aware that he was not going to leave the tonghouse alive. Not unless he reached the door to the joss room in time to shut it and hold it closed against the swarm of hatchetmen.

After firing his last shot he turned and ran full tilt for the door. His foot caught on the sill as he rushed through and he tumbled to the floor. The horror of knowing that he was about to be hacked to death shot strength into his legs but he slipped as he started to rise and knew he was done for.

As he rolled, tensing for the first ax strike, preparing a last stand with his bare hands, he was startled by the sound of gunfire, followed immediately by shouts and screams of pain. He looked up and saw the old man's turbaned Indian wielding a huge scimitar that lopped off heads and arms with slashing swipes, while the driver hacked away with a cutlass. The old man himself stood in the thick of it, firing a round-handled, long-barreled Mauser at any of the hatchet man who slipped past his front line.

Brannigan pawed fresh shells from his jacket pocket and began to reload. But the melee was over before he finished. He sat up and looked around. More than joss-stick smoke hung in the air; blood had spattered the feathered walls and pooled on the floor. The old man and the Indian were unscathed; the driver was bleeding from a gash on his right arm but didn't seem to notice.

"What…how…?"

The old man looked at him. "I sensed you weren't telling us everything you knew, so we followed you. Good thing too, I'd say."

Brannigan nodded as he struggled to his feet. He felt shaky, unsteady.

"Thank you. I owe you my–"

"Is she here?" the old man said. "Have you seen her?"

"I have her right here, Oliver," said a sibilant, accented voice.

Brannigan turned and raised his pistol as a motley group filed into the small room: a green-eyed, turquoise-robed Chinaman entered, followed by a trio of gangly, brutal-looking, dark-skinned lugs dressed in loin cloths and nothing else; one carried a red-haired girl in his arms; two black-pajama'd tongsters brought up the rear, one thin, one fat, the latter with his hands tied behind his back and looking as if he'd wound up on the wrong end of a billy club.

The lead Chinaman spoke again. "I feared you might have been drawn into this."

"So it's you, doctor," the old man said. At least Brannigan knew part of his name now: Oliver. "Striking at me through my child? I knew you were ruthless but–"

"Do not insult me, Oliver. I would gladly cut out your heart, but I would not break it."

The doctor – doctor of what? Brannigan wondered – removed a bony, long-fingered hand from within a sleeve and gestured to the loin-clothed crew. The one carrying the little girl stepped forward and handed her over to Oliver. She looked drugged but as the old man took her in his arms, her eyes fluttered open. Brannigan saw her smile

The word was a whisper. "Daddy."

Tears rimmed Oliver's eyes as he looked down at her, then back to the doctor. "I don't understand."

"This was not my doing." Without looking he flicked a finger toward the fat, bound tongster. "This doomed one broke an agreement."

"I thought I left you back in Hong Kong. When was it…?"

"Three years ago. I understand you recently closed your factory there."

He nodded. "The political climate in the Far East has accomplished what you could not. I'm gathering my chicks closer to the nest, you might say. A storm is brewing and I want to be properly positioned when it strikes."

The doctor's smile was acid. "To profiteer, as usual."

Oliver shrugged. "Nothing wrong with doing well while doing good."

Who were these two? Brannigan wondered. They stood, each with his own personal army, like ancient mythical enemies facing each other across a bottomless divide.

"And what of you, doctor?" Oliver continued. "With your homeland being invaded, why are you here?"

"You heard what the Japanese dogs did in Nanking?"

"Yes. Ghastly. I'm sorry."

"Then you can understand why I am here. To raise money from the underworld for weapons to repel the insects."

Oliver's faint smile looked bitter. "And all along you thought the enemy was people like me."

"You still are. My goal remains unchanged: To drive all foreigners from Chinese soil. I will admit, however, that I singled out the white western world as the threat, never realizing that a yellow-skinned neighbor would prove a far more vicious foe."

Something the doctor had said rang through Brannigan's brain: *To raise money from he underworld…*that could only mean–

He pointed his pistol at the green-robed chink. "You're the Mandarin! You're–"

The green eyes glanced his way and the pure malevolence in them clogged the words in Brannigan's throat. Before he could clear it, Oliver pointed to the bound chink and spoke.

"I'll take him from here. My associates and I have a score to settle."

"No, he is mine. He broke his word to me. I have experts in the Thousand Cuts. He will die long after he wishes to, I promise."

Brannigan couldn't believe his ears. These two acted like laws unto themselves. It was like listening to two sovereign nations states argue over extradition of a prisoner.

"Hey, wait just a minute, you two." He stepped closer to the Mandarin. "Neither of you is going to do anything." The green eyes turned on him again. "I'm arresting you and your tongster buddy here for–"

Something smashed against the back of Brannigan's skull, dropping him to his knees. He tried to regain his feet but the edges of his vision went blurry and he toppled forward into darkness.

*

Jiang Zhifu poised his fist over the fallen detective's neck and looked to the master for permission to finish the worm. The master nodded. But as Jiang raised his hand for the deathblow a shot rang out and a bullet plowed into the feathered wall beside him.

"That will be enough," said the man called Oliver.

The master motioned Jiang back toward Yu and he obeyed, albeit reluctantly. He was confused. Who was this white devil to give orders in the master's presence, and have the master acquiesce? Although this Oliver and the master seemed to be old enemies, the master treated him as an equal.

Something became clear to Jiang. It must have been because of this man that the master had sent Jiang to the Fairmont Hotel where he'd been instructed to ask a certain question of the kitchen staff. When Jiang returned with word that yes, meals were indeed being delivered to the penthouse suite, the master had changed his plans.

Jiang looked at the little red-haired girl in Oliver's arms. Yu had brought all this to pass by abducting her. The master had hinted that consequences most dire and relentless would befall anyone even remotely connected with harming that child.

Jiang had doubted that, but looking around the joss room now, he believed. So many of his tong brothers dead, shot or hacked to pieces. He and Yu were the only two members of Yan Yuap left alive in the house. Jiang would have to leave and return at dawn with the rest of the members, feigning shock at the carnage here.

"As I was saying, Oliver, before we were interrupted, this worthless one is mine to deal with, but if you wish I can have some expert seamstresses stitch his skin back together and make you a gift of it."

"Thanks for the offer," he said but did not look grateful. "I think I'll pass on that."

"Then I shall nail it to the wall of this tonghouse as a warning."

Jiang jumped as a slurred voice said, "The only thing you'll be doing is looking the wrong way through the bars of a jail cell."

Aiii! The detective was conscious again. He must have a skull as thick as the walls of the Imperial Palace!

The master spoke without a trace of fear. "You have at most six shots, detective. My dacoits will be upon you before you can shoot all of them."

The detective leveled his pistol at the master's heart.

"Yeah, but the first one will go into you."

Yu started to move forward, crying, "Yes! Arrest me! Please!"

But Jiang yanked him back and struck him across the throat – not a killing blow, just enough to silence him.

The master only smiled. "You may arrest me if you wish, detective, but that will doom the ten women this bloated slug collected for export."

The detective's eyes widened. "Ten? Good Christ, where are they?"

"In a ship in the harbor, moored at Pier Twelve. A ship wired to explode at midnight."

"You're lying!"

"He doesn't lie, Brannigan," said Oliver. "Over our years of conflict I've learned that the doctor is capable of just about anything, but he never lies."

"If you look at your watch," the master said, "you will see that you have time to bring me to your precinct house or rush to the harbor and save the women. But not both."

Jiang could see the detective's resolve wavering.

The master continued in a silky, almost seductive voice. "May I suggest the former course? Think what bringing in the mysterious and notorious Mandarin will do for your career. It will guarantee you the promotion you most surely desire."

The detective looked to Oliver. "Will you hold him here until–?"

The older man cut him off with a quick shake of his head. "This is your show, kid." He looked down at the child stirring in his arms. "I have what I came for. You choose."

He backed toward the door.

"Damn you all!"

Then he turned and ran.

Jiang knew that if the young detective broke all speed records, he might reach the docks in time. Fortunately for him, he would meet little resistance aboard ship; most of the crew had deserted once word leaked out that Yu had displeased the Mandarin.

When the detective was gone, Oliver smiled. "Dear doctor, you never fail to find interesting ways to test people. I'm glad he chose what he did, otherwise I'd have had to send my associates to the waterfront. As it is, I've got someone here who needs some attending to, and I have a call to make."

He turned to go, then turned back.

"Oh, and those weapons your people need…if you have trouble buying through the usual channels, call me. I'm sure we can work something out."

And then the master shocked Jiang by doing the unthinkable. He inclined his head toward this man named Oliver.

*

There's still a chance, Brannigan thought as he jumped behind the wheel of his radio car.

He'd call the station and send a squad of cars to the docks while he returned to the tonghouse and collared the Mandarin.

But when he snatched the microphone from its holder he noticed the frayed end of its coiled wire dangling in the air.

"Damn!"

He tossed the useless piece of garbage against the passenger door. No options left. He started to car, threw it into gear, and floored the gas pedal. He didn't think he could make it, but he was going to try.

Traffic was light and with his siren howling he reached the docks in five minutes. He found Pier Twelve and raced up the gangplank of a rustbucket freighter, his pistol held before him.

He reached the deck and, with only that wash of light from the city behind him for illumination, looked around. The tub looked deserted. Two of the three cargo hatches lay open. He ran to the third and rapped on it with the gun butt.

"Hello! Anyone in there?"

The muffled chorus of female voices from below was a sweet symphony. He found the fasteners, released them, and pulled off the cover.

"Detective Brad Brannigan," he said into the square of darkness below him, and the words had never sounded so good on his tongue. "Let's get you gals out of there."

As the captives shouted, cried, and sobbed with relief, Brannigan grabbed the rope ladder coiled by the hatch and tossed it over the edge.

"Squeeze the minutes, girls! We haven't got much time."

As the first climbed into view, a rather plain blonde, he grabbed her arm and hauled her onto the deck.

"Run! Get down the gangplank and keep going!"

He repeated this with each of the girls – amazingly, all blondes.

"I thought there were ten of you," he said as he helped the ninth over the rim.

"Margot hurt her ankle when they grabbed her. She can't climb up."

Hell and damn. Margot Kachmar, the one who started all this for him. He wished he could see his watch. How much time did he have left, if any?

Didn't matter. He hadn't finished the job.

He directed number nine to the gangway, then leaned over the rim and called into the darkness below.

"Margot? Are you near the ladder?"

"Yes, but–"

"No buts. Put your good foot on a rung and hold on tight."

"O-okay." He felt the ropes tighten. "I'm on. Now what?"

"I bring you up."

Brannigan sat on the deck, braced his feet against the hatch rim, and began hauling on the rope ladder. The coarse coils burned his palms and his back protested, but he kept at it, pulling rung after ropy rung up and over the edge until he saw a pair of hands grip the rim.

"Keep coming!" he shouted, maintaining tension on the rope.

When her face was visible and she had both elbows over the rim, he grabbed her and hauled her onto the deck.

"Oh, thank you!" she sobbed as she looked at the city. "I'd given up hope of ever seeing home again!"

"Don't thank me yet." He lifted her into his arms and carried her toward the gangway. "C'mon, kiddo. Your daddy's waiting for you."

His haste gave him a bad moment on the gangway as he slipped halfway down and nearly fell off. He was just stepping onto the dock with his burden safe and unharmed when a bright flash lit up the night.

"Hold it!" a man's voice said. "One more!"

The purple afterimage of the flash blotted out whoever was talking.

"What?"

A second flash and then another voice saying, "Joe Stenson from the *Chronicle*. You're name's Brannigan, right?"

"Yes, but–"

"That's with a double 'n'?"

"Get out of here!" Brannigan shouted as he began carrying Margot away from the ship. "The ship's going to blow at midnight!"

"Blow?"

"As in explode!"

"But it's already after midnight," Stenson said.

Brannigan slowed for a few steps. Had he been duped? Then he remembered what Oliver had said about the Mandarin always keeping his word and resumed his frantic pace.

"Just get away from the ship!"

"If you say so."

Stenson was pacing him to his left. A photographer ambled on his right.

"How come you two are down here?" Brannigan asked.

"Got a tip. Guy didn't give his name, just told me to get down to Pier Twelve if I wanted to catch a hero cop in action, and am I ever glad I listened. The girls told me what happened to them, and that picture of you carrying this little lady down the gangplank – hoo boy, if that's not front page stuff, I'll quit and open a flower shop."

Ahead Brannigan could see the rest of the girls waiting near the street, cheering when they saw he had Margot. He set her down on the curb and they all gathered around, hugging her, hugging him, while the photographer flashed away.

"What was that about the ship exploding at midnight?" Stenson said. "Were you–?"

And then the pavement shook and the night lit up like day as huge explosions ripped through the old freighter, rupturing her hull and shooting hundred-foot columns of flame up the hatches.

Stenson turned to his photographer. "Are you getting this, Louie?"

"I'm getting it, Joe. Am I ever getting it!"

The adrenaline began seeping away then, leaving Brannigan fagged. He'd missed collaring the Mandarin, but looking at these ten girls, all alive and well because of him, he couldn't help but feel on top of the world.

But who in the world had called the *Chronicle*?

He sensed motion behind him and turned to see a Silver Rolls Royce gliding by. A little red-haired girl smiled and waved from the rear window before the car was swallowed by the fog.

Part of the Game

"You have been brought to attention of a most illustrious one," Jiang Zhifu said.

The Chinaman wore long black cotton pajamas with a high collar and onyx-buttoned front. He'd woven his hair into a braid that snaked out from beneath a traditional black skullcap. His eyes were as shiny and black as his onyx buttons and, typical of his kind, gave nothing away.

Detective Sergeant Hank Sorenson smiled. "I guess the Mandarin heard about my little show at Wang's pai gow parlor last night."

Jiang's mug remained typically inscrutable. "I not mention such a one."

"Didn't have to. Tell him I want to meet him."

Jiang blinked. Got him! Direct speech always set these chinks back on their heels.

Hank let his cup of tea cool on the small table between them. He'd pretend to take a sip or two but not a drop would pass his lips. He doubted anyone down here would make a move against a bull, but you could never be sure where the Mandarin was concerned.

He tried to get a bead on this coolie. A call in the night from someone saying he was Jiang Zhifu, a "representative" – these chinks made him laugh – of an important man in Chinatown. He didn't have to say who. Hank knew. The chink said they must meet to discuss important matters of mutual interest. At the Jade Moon. Ten A.M.

Hank knew the place – next to a Plum Street joss house – and he'd arrived early. First thing he'd done was check out the rear alley. All clear. Inside he'd chosen a corner table near the rear door and seated himself with his back to the wall.

The Jade Moon wasn't exactly high end as Chinkytown restaurants went: dirty floors, smudged tumblers, chipped lacquer on the doors and trim, ratty looking paper lanterns dangling from the exposed beams.

Not the kind of place he'd expect to meet a minion of the mysterious and powerful and ever-elusive Mandarin.

The Mandarin didn't run Chinatown's rackets. He had a better deal: He skimmed them. Never got his hands dirty except with the money that crossed them. Dope, prostitution, gambling…the Mandarin took a cut of everything.

How he'd pulled that off was a bigger mystery than his identity. Hank had dealt with the tongs down here – tough muggs one and all.

Not the sort you'd figure to hand over part of their earnings without a fight. But they did.

Well, maybe there'd been a dust up and they lost. But if that was what had happened, it must have been fought out of sight, because he hadn't heard a word about it.

Hank had been running the No-Tickee-No-Shirtee beat for SFPD since 1935 – three years here and he'd yet to find anyone who'd ever seen the Mandarin. And they weren't just saying they'd never seen them – they meant it. If his time down here had taught him anything, it was you never ask a Chink a direct question. You couldn't treat them like regular people. You had to approach everything on an angle. They were devious, crafty, always dodging and weaving, always ducking the question and avoiding an answer.

He'd developed a nose for their lies, but had never caught a whiff of deceit when he'd asked about the Mandarin. Even when he'd played rough with a character or two, they didn't know who the big guy was, where he was, or what he looked like.

It had taken Hank a while to reach the astonishing conclusion that they didn't *want* to know. And that had taken him aback. Chinks were gossipmongers – yak-yak-yak in their singsong voices, trading rumors and tidbits like a bunch of old biddies. For them to avoid talking about someone meant they were afraid.

Even the little people were afraid. That said something for the Mandarin's reach.

Hank had to admit he was impressed, but hardly afraid. He wasn't a chink.

Jiang had arrived exactly at ten, kowtowing before seating himself

"Even if I knew of such a one," the Chinaman said, "I am sure he not meet with you. He send emissary, just as my master send me."

Hank smiled. These chinks…

"Okay, if that's the way we're going to play it, you tell your master that I want a piece of his pie."

Jiang frowned. "Pie?"

"His cream. His skim. His payoff from all the opium and dolla-dolla girls and gambling down here."

"Ah so." Jiang nodded. "My master realize that such arrangement is part of everyday business, but one such as he not sully hands with such. He suggest you contact various sources of activities that interest you and make own arrangements with those establishments."

Hank leaned forward and put on his best snarl.

"Listen, you yellow-faced lug. I don't have time to go around bracing every penny-ante operation down here. I know your boss gets a cut from all of them, so I want a cut from *him*! Clear?"

"I afraid that quite impossible."

"*Nothing* is impossible!" He leaned back. "But I'm a reasonable man. I don't want it all. I don't even want half of it all. I'll settle for an even split of just his gambling take."

Jiang smiled. "This a jest, yes?"

"I'm serious. Dead serious. He can keep everything from the dope and the heifer dens. I want half of the Mandarin's gambling take."

Hank knew that was where the money was in Chinatown. Opium was big down here, but gambling…these coolies gambled on anything and everything. They had their games, sure – parlors for fan-tan, mah-jongg, pai gow, sic bo, pak kop piu, and others – but they didn't stop there. Numbers had a huge take. He'd seen slips collected day and night on street corners all over the quarter. Write down three numbers, hand them in with your money, and pray the last three Dow Jones digits matched yours at the end of trading.

They'd bet on just about any damn thing, even the weather.

They didn't bother to hide their games either. They'd post the hours of operation on their doors, and some even had touts standing out front urging people inside. Gambling was in their blood, and gambling was where the money was, so gambling was where Hank wanted to be.

No, make that *would* be.

Jiang shook his head and began to rise. "So sorry, Detective Sorenson, but–"

Hank sprang from his chair and grabbed the front of Jiang's black top.

"Listen, chink-boy! This is not negotiable! One way or another I'm going to be part of the game down here. Get that? A big part. Or else there'll *be* no game. I'll bring in squad after squad and we'll collar every numbers coolie and shut down every lousy parlor in the quarter – mah-jongg, sic bo, you name it, it's history. And then what will your boss's take be? What's a hundred percent of nothing, huh?"

He jerked Jiang closer and backhanded him across the face, then shoved him against the wall.

"Tell him he either gets smart or he gets nothing!"

Hank might have said more, but the look of murderous rage in Jiang's eyes stalled the words in his throat.

"Dog!" the chink whispered through clenched teeth. "You have made this one lose face before these people!"

Hank looked around the suddenly silent restaurant. Diners and waiters alike stood frozen, gawking at him. But Hank Sorenson wasn't about to be cowed by a bunch of coolies.

He jabbed a finger at Jiang. "Who do you think you are, calling me a–?"

Jiang made a slashing motion with his hand. "I am servant of one who would not wipe his slippers on your back. You make this one lose face, and that mean you make *him* lose face. Woe to you, Detective Sorenson."

Without warning he let out a yelp and slammed the knife-edge of his hand onto the table, then turned and walked away.

He was halfway to the door when the table fell apart.

Hank stood in shock, staring down at the pile of splintered wood. What the–?

Never mind that now. He gathered his wits and looked around. He wanted out of here, but didn't want to walk past all those staring eyes. They might see how he was shaking inside.

That table…if Jiang could do that to wood, what could he do to a neck?

Fending off that unsettling thought, he left by the back door. He took a deep breath of putrid, back-alley air as he stepped outside. The late morning sun hadn't risen high enough yet to break up the shadows here.

Well, he'd delivered his message. And the fact that Jiang had struck the table instead of him only reinforced what he already knew: no worry about bull busting down here. No chink would dare lay a hand on a buzzer-carrying member of the SFPD. They knew what would happen in their neighborhoods if anyone ever did something like that.

He sighed as he walked toward the street. At least during his time in the restaurant he'd been thinking of something other than Tempest. But now she came back to him. Her face, her form, her voice…oh, that voice.

Tempest, Tempest, Tempest…

*

Jiang knelt before the Mandarin and pressed his forehead against the stone floor.

"I should have killed the dog for his insult to you, Venerable,"

Instead of his usual Cantonese, Jiang spoke in Mandarin – fittingly, the language the Mandarin preferred.

"No," the master said in his soft, sibilant voice. "You did well not to harm him. We must find a more indirect path to deal with such a one. Sit, Jiang."

"Thank you, Illustrious."

Jiang raised his head from the floor but remained kneeling, daring only a furtive peek at his master. Many times he had seen the one known throughout Chinatown as the Mandarin – not even Jiang knew his true name – but that did not lessen the wonder of his appearance.

A high-shouldered man standing tall and straight with his hands folded inside the sleeves of his embroidered emerald robe; a black skull cap covered the thin hair that fringed his high, domed forehead. Jiang marveled as ever at his light green eyes that almost seemed to glow.

He did not know if his master was a true mandarin – he had heard someone address him once as "Doctor" – or merely called such because of the dialect he preferred. He did know the master spoke many languages. He'd heard him speak English, French, German, and even a low form of Hindi to the dacoits in his employ.

For all the wealth flowing through his coffers, the master lived frugally. The money went back to the homeland for to serve a purpose higher than mere creature comfort.

"So this miserable offspring of a maggot demands half the gambling tribute. Wishes to be – how did he put it? – 'part of the game?' "

"Yes, Magnificent."

The master closed his eyes. "Part of the game…part of the game…by all means we must grant his wish."

Jiang spent the ensuing moments of silence in a whirlpool of confusion. The master…giving in to the cockroach's demands? Unthinkable! And yet he'd said–

An upward glance showed the master's eyes open again and a hint of a smile curving his thin lips.

"Yes, that is it. We shall make him part of the game."

Jiang had seen that smile before. He knew what usually followed. It made him three-times glad that he was not Detective Sorenson.

*

Hank held up his double-breasted tuxedo and inspected it, paying special attention to the wide satin lapels. No spots. Good. He could get a few more wears before sending it for cleaning.

As always, he was struck by the incongruity of a tux in his shabby two-room apartment. Well, it should look out of place. It had cost him a month's rent.

All for Tempest.

That babe was costing him a fortune. Trouble was, he didn't have a fortune. But the Chinatown games would fix that.

He shook his head. That kind of scheme would have been unthinkable back in the days when he was a fresh bull. And if not for Tempest it would still be.

But a woman can change everything. A woman can turn you inside out and upside down.

Tempest was one of those women.

He remembered the first time he'd seen her at the Serendipity Club. Like getting gut punched. She wasn't just a choice piece of calico; she had the kind of looks that could put your conscience on hold. Then she'd stepped up to the mike and…a voice like an angel. When Hank heard her sing "I've Got You Under My Skin," that was it. He was gone. He'd heard Doris Lessing sing it a hundred times on the radio, but Tempest…Tempest made him feel like she was singing to him.

Hank had stayed on through the last show. When she finished he followed her – a flash of his buzzer got him past the geezer guarding the backstage door – and asked her out. A cop wasn't the usual stage-door Johnny and so she'd said okay.

Hank had gone all out to impress her, and they'd been on the town half a dozen times so far. She'd tapped him out without letting him get to first base. He knew he wasn't the only guy she dated – he'd spied her out with a couple rich cake eaters – but Hank wasn't the sharing kind. Trouble was, to get an exclusive on her was going to take moolah. Lots of it.

And he was going to get lots of it. A steady stream…

He yawned. What with playing the bon vivant by night and the soft heel by day, he wasn't getting much sleep.

He dropped onto the bed, rolled onto his back, and closed his eyes. Tempest didn't go on for another couple of hours, so a catnap would be just the ticket. He was slipping into that mellow, drowsy state just before dropping off to sleep when he felt a sharp pain in his left shoulder, like he'd been stabbed with an ice pick.

As he bolted out of bed Hank felt something wriggling against his undershirt. He reached back and felt little legs – *lots* of little legs. Fighting a sick revulsion he grabbed it and pulled. It writhed and twisted in his hand but held fast to his skin. Hank clenched his teeth and yanked.

As the thing came free, pain like he'd never known or imagined exploded in his shoulder, driving him to his knees. He dropped the wriggling creature and slapped a hand over the live coal embedded in his shoulder. Through tear-blurred vision he saw a scarlet millipede at least eight inches long scurrying away across the floor.

"What the–?"

He reached for something, anything to use against it. He grabbed a shoe and smashed it down on the thing. The heel caught the back half of its body and Hank felt it squish with a crunch.

The front half spasmed, reared up, then tore free and darted under the door and out into the hallway before he could get a second shot.

Hell with it! His shoulder was killing him.

He brought his hand away and found blood on his palm. Not much but enough to shake him. He struggled to his feet and stepped into his tiny bathroom. The bright bulb over the speckled mirror picked up the beads of sweat on his brow.

He was shaking. What was that thing? He'd never seen anything like it. And how had it got in his room, in his *bed*, for Christ sake?

He half turned and angled his shoulder toward the mirror. The size of the bite surprised him – only a couple of punctures within a small smear of blood. From the ferocity of the pain he'd expected something like a .38 entry wound.

The burning started to subside. Thank God. He balled up some toilet tissue and dabbed at the wound. Looky there. Stopped bleeding already.

He went back to the front room and looked at the squashed remains of the thing. Damn. It looked like something you'd find in a jungle. Like the Amazon.

How'd it wind up in San Francisco?

Probably crawled off a boat.

Hank shuddered as he noticed couple of the rearmost legs still twitching.

He kicked it into a corner.

*

"The usual table, detective?" Maurice said with a practiced smile.

Hank nodded and followed the Serendipity's maitre d' to a second-level table for two just off the dance floor.

"Thank you, Maurice."

He passed him a fin he could barely afford as they shook hands. He ordered a scotch and water and started a tab. This was the last night he'd be able to do this until the Mandarin came across with some lucre.

He shook his head. All it takes is money. You don't have to be smart or even good looking, all you need is lots of do-re-mi and everybody wants to know you. Suddenly you're Mr. Popularity.

As Hank sipped his drink and waited for Tempest to take the stage, he felt his shoulder start to burn. Damn. Not again. The pain had lasted only half an hour after the bite and then felt as good as new. But now it was back and growing stronger.

Heat spread from the bite, flowing through him, burning his skin, breaking him out in a sweat. Suddenly he had no strength. His hands, his arms, his legs…all rubbery. The glass slipped from his fingers, spilling scotch down the pleated front of his shirt.

The room rocked and swayed as he tried to rise, but his legs wouldn't hold him. He felt himself falling, saw the curlicue pattern of the rug rushing at him.

Then nothing.

*

Hank opened his eyes and found himself looking up at a woman in white. She looked about fifty. He looked down. More white. Sheets. He was in a bed.

"Where–?"

She flashed a reassuring smile. "You're in St. Luke's and you're going to be just fine. I'll let your doctor know you're awake."

Hank watched her bustle out the door. He felt dazed. The last thing he remembered –

That bite from the millipede – poison. Had to be.

The pain had tapered to a dull ache, but he still felt weak as a kitty.

A balding man with a gray mustache strode through the door and stepped up to the bed. He wore a white coat with a pair of pens in the breast pocket and carried a clipboard under his arm.

"Detective Sorenson," he said, extending his hand, "I'm Doctor Cranston, and you've got quite a boil on your back."

"Boil?"

"Yes. A pocket of infection in your skin. You shouldn't let those things go. The infection can seep into your system and make you very ill. How long have you had it?"

Hank pulled the hospital gown off his shoulder and gaped at the golf-ball-size red swelling.

"That wasn't there when I put on my shirt tonight."

Dr. Cranston harrumphed. "Of course it was. These things don't reach that size in a matter of hours."

A flash of anger cut through Hank's fuzzy brain. "This one did. I was bitten there by a giant bug around seven o'clock."

Cranston smoothed his mustache. "Really? What kind of bug?"

"Don't know. Never seen anything like it."

"Well, be that as it may, we'll open it up, clean out the infection, and you'll be on your way in no time."

Hank hoped so.

*

Bared to the waist, Hank lay on his belly while the nurse swabbed his shoulder with some sort of antiseptic.

"You may feel a brief sting as I break the skin, but once we relieve the pressure from all that pus inside, it'll be like money from home."

Hank looked up and saw the scalpel in Cranston's hand. He turned away.

"Do it."

Cranston was half right: Hank felt the sting, but no relief.

He heard Cranston mutter, "Well, this is one for Ripley's."

Hank didn't like the sound of that.

"What's wrong?"

"Most odd. There's no pus in this, only serous fluid."

"What's serous fluid?"

"A clear amber fluid – just like you'd see seeping from a burn blister. Most odd, most odd." Cranston, cleared his throat. "I believe we'll keep you overnight."

"But I can't–"

"You must. You're too weak to be sent home. And I want to look into this insect. What did it look like?"

"Send someone to my place and you'll find its back half."

"I believe I'll do just that."

*

Two days cooped up in a hospital room hadn't made Hank any better. He had to get out to seal the deal with the Mandarin. But how? He was able to stand and walk – shuffle was more like it – but he still felt so weak. And the pounds were dropping off him like leaves from a tree.

The boil or whatever it was had gone from a lump to a big open sore that wept fluid all day.

He was sitting on the edge of the bed, looking out at the fogged-in city when Cranston trundled in.

"Well, we've identified that millipede."

Here was the first good news since he'd been bitten.

"What is it?"

"The entomologists over at Berkley gave it a name as long as your arm. Other than that they weren't much help. Said it was very, very rare, and that only a few have ever been seen. Couldn't imagine how it managed to travel from the rain forests of Borneo to your bed."

"Borneo," Hank said. Everybody had heard of the Wild Man from Borneo but… "Just where the hell is Borneo?"

"It's an island in the South China Sea."

"Did you say South *China* Sea?"

Cranston nodded. "Yes. Why? Is that important?"

Hank didn't answer. He couldn't. It was all clear now.

Good Christ…China…

The Mandarin had sent his reply to Hank's demand.

"There's, um, something else you should know."

Cranston's tone snapped Hank's head up. The doctor looked uneasy. His gaze wandered to the window.

"You mean it gets worse?" Cranston's nod sent a sick, cold spike through Hank's gut. "Okay. Give it to me."

Cranston took a breath. "The millipede may or may not have injected you with venom, but that's not the problem." His voice trailed off.

Hank didn't know if he wanted to hear this.

"What *is* the problem then?"

"You remember when we did a scraping of the wound?"

"How could I forget?"

"Well, we did a microscopic examination and found what, um, appear to be eggs."

Hank's gut twisted into a knot.

"Eggs!"

"Yes."

"Did you get them all?"

"We don't know. They're quite tiny. But we'll go back in and do another scraping, deeper this time. But you should know…"

"Know what?"

Cranston's gaze remained fixed on the window.

"They're hatching."

*

Next day, one of the green soft heels, a grade-one detective named Brannigan, stopped by to ask about Chinatown. He'd been assigned to look for a missing white girl last seen down there. He was asking about the Mandarin. Hank warned him away, even went so far as to show him the big, weeping ulcer on his shoulder.

Suddenly he was seized by a coughing fit, one that went on and on until he hacked up a big glob of bright red phlegm. The blood shocked him, but the sight of the little things wriggling in the gooey mass completely unnerved him.

"Oh, God!" he cried to Brannigan. "Call the doctor! Get the nurse in here! Hurry!"

The eggs had hatched and they were in his lungs! How had they gotten into his lungs?

Sick horror pushed a sob to his throat. He tried to hold it back until Brannigan was out the door. He didn't think he made it.

*

Hank stared at the stranger in the bathroom mirror.

"It's not unprecedented," Cranston had said. "Larva of the ascaris round worm, for instance, get into the circulation and migrate through the lung. But we've no experience with this species."

He saw sunken cheeks, glassy, feverish eyes, sallow, sweaty skin as pale as the sink, and knew he was looking at a dead man.

Why hadn't he just played it straight – or at least only a little bent – and taken a payoff here and there from the bigger gambling parlors? Why had he tried to go for the big score?

Three days since he'd coughed up those first baby millipedes. Now he was hacking them up every day. That thing must have laid thousands, maybe tens of thousands of eggs in his shoulder. Her babies were sitting in his lungs, sucking off his blood as it passed through, eating him alive from the inside.

And nobody could do a damn thing about it.

He started to cry. He'd been doing that a lot lately. He couldn't help it. He felt so damn helpless.

The phone started to ring. Probably Hanrahan. The chief had been down to see him once and had never returned. Hank didn't blame him. Probably couldn't stand looking the near-empty shell he'd become.

Hank shuffled to the bedside and picked up the receiver.

"Yeah."

"Ah, Detective Sorenson," said a voice he immediately recognized. "So glad you are still with us."

A curse leaped to his lips but he bit it back. He didn't need any more bugs in his bed.

"No thanks to you."

"Ah, so. A most regrettable turn of events, but also most inevitable, given such circumstances."

"Did you call to gloat?"

"Ah, no. I call to offer you your wish."

Hank froze as a tremor of hope ran through his ravaged body. He was almost afraid to ask.

"You can cure me?"

"Come again to Jade Moon at three o'clock this day and your wish shall be granted."

The line went dead.

*

The cab stopped in front of the Jade moon. Hank needed just about every ounce of strength to haul himself out of the rear seat.

The nurses had wailed, Dr. Cranston had blustered, but they couldn't keep him if he wanted to go. When they saw how serious he was, the nurses dug up a cane to help him walk.

He leaned on that cane now and looked around. The sidewalk in front of the restaurant was packed with chinks, and every one of them staring at him. Not just staring – pointing and whispering too.

Couldn't blame them. He must be quite a sight in his wrinkled, oversize tux. Used to fit like tailor made, but now it hung on him like a coat on a scarecrow. But he'd had no choice. This had been the only clothing in his hospital room closet.

He stepped up on the curb and stood swaying. For a few seconds he feared he might fall. The cane saved him.

He heard the singsong babble increase and noticed that the crowd was growing, with more chinks pouring in from all directions, so many that they blocked the street. All staring, pointing, whispering.

Obviously Jiang had put out the word to come see the bad joss that befell anyone who went against the Mandarin.

Well, Hank thought as he began his shuffle toward the restaurant door, enjoy the show, you yellow bastards.

The crowd parted for him and watched as he struggled to open the door. No one stepped up to help. Someone inside pushed it open and pointed to the rear of the restaurant.

Hank saw Jiang sitting at the same table where they'd first met. Only this time Jiang's back was to the wall. He didn't kowtow, didn't even rise when Hank reached the table.

"Sit, Detective Sorenson," he said, indicating the other chair.

He looked exactly the same a last time: same black pajamas, same skullcap, same braid, same expressionless face.

Hank, on the other hand…

"I'll stand."

"Ah so, you not looking well. I must tell you that if you fall this one not help you up."

Hank knew if he went down he'd never be able to get up on his own. What then? Would all the chinks outside be paraded past him for another look?

He dropped into the chair. That was when he noticed something like an ebony cigar box sitting before Jiang.

"What's that? Another bug?"

Jiang pushed it toward Hank.

"Ah no, very much opposite. This fight your infestation."

Hank closed his eyes and bit back a sob. A cure…was he really offering a cure? But he knew there had to be a catch.

"What do I have to do for it?"

"Must take three time a day."

Hank couldn't believe it.

"That's it? No strings?"

Jiang shook his head. "No, as you say, strings." He opened the box to reveal dozens of cigarette-size red paper cylinders. "Merely break one open three time a day and breathe fine powder within."

As much as Hank wanted to believe, his mind still balked at the possibility that this could be on the level.

"That's it? Three times a day and I'll be cured?"

"I not promise cure. I say it fight infestation."

"What's the difference? And what is this stuff?"

"Eggs of tiny parasite."

"A parasite!" Hank pushed the box away. "Not on your life!"

"This is true. Not on my life – on *your* life."

"I don't get it."

"There is order to universe, Detective Sorenson: Everything must feed. Something must die so that other may live. And it is so with these powdery parasite eggs. Humans do not interest them. They grow only in larvae that infest your lung. They devour host from inside and leave own eggs in carcass."

"Take a parasite to kill a parasite? That's crazy."

"Not crazy. It is poetry."

"How do I know it won't just make me sicker."

Jiang smiled, the first time he'd changed his expression. "Sicker? How much more sick can Detective Sorenson be?"

"I don't get it. You half kill me, then you offer to cure me. What's the deal? Your Mandarin wants a pet cop, is that it?"

"I know of no Mandarin. And once again, I not promise cure, only *chance* of cure."

Hank's hopes tripped but didn't fall.

"You mean it might not work?"

"It matter of balance, Detective. Have larvae gone too far for parasite to kill all in time? Or does Detective Sorenson still have strength enough left to survive? That is where fun come in."

"Fun? You call this *fun*?"

"Fun not for you or for this one. Fun for everyone else because my master decide grant wish you made."

"Wish? What wish?"

"To be part of game – your very words. Remember?"

Hank remembered, but…

"I'm not following you."

"All of Chinatown taking bet on you."

"On me?"

"Yes. Even money on whether live or die. And among those who believe you soon join ancestors, a lottery on when." Another smile. "You have your wish, Detective Sorenson. You now very much part of game. Ah so, you *are* game."

Hank wanted to scream, wanted to bolt from his chair and wipe the smirk off Jiang's rotten yellow face. But that was only a dream. The best he could do was sob and let the tears stream down his cheeks as he reached into the box for one of the paper cylinders.

Dragon's Tongue

"He's here," I said, dropping into the chair opposite the Old Man's desk.

Morning sunlight – what little could filter through the thick fog – lit the window behind him. The Old Man had his jacket off and sat in his shirtsleeves.

He looked around. "Where?"

"In town."

"Swell. Mind telling me who?"

"That Lord of Strange Deaths character."

"Lord of Strange–?" The Old Man leaned back, hooked his thumbs in his suspenders, and stared at me. "You been drinking?"

"Hell, no. At least not yet."

"The sun out there in Arizona fried your brain, then?"

I'd been stinging after letting that green cop Brannigan do an end run around me on the Kachmar case. The Old Man would have dearly loved the publicity that would have come with one of his guys rescuing those girls, and wasn't happy about me missing out. What can I day? The kid got lucky. So to make nice-nice, I'd agreed to chase down a runaway heiress someplace in the desert – a crummy Phoenix suburb called Scottsdale. The light and air out there had hurt my eyes – everything so bright and sharp and clear. San Francisco fog could be annoying at times, but it had looked good on my return. I'd just returned.

"I made sure I wore my hat."

"Then what in blazes are you talking about?"

"Remember that limey a couple years back who hired us to find his stolen whatchamacallit?"

"Haven't a clue."

"Yeah, you do. Because he paid us three times the daily rate."

"Oh, yeah. Him." I knew mentioning the triple rate would jog the Old Man's memory. He didn't forget money. He jabbed a finger my way. "And as I recall he wanted you and only you."

I deadpanned it. "Yeah. He knew quality."

"He's dead, as I recall."

"Yeah, bitten by a puff adder in his London digs."

"Imagine that. Talk about a freak accident."

"Accident? A deadly snake somehow makes its way from Africa to a London apartment and kills a guy. I'd call that a strange death, wouldn't you?"

The Old Man shifted in his seat. "I suppose."

"And this same limey just so happened to hire us – me, specifically – to hunt down some mystery chink who was known to the other

London chinks as 'the Lord of Strange Deaths.' Coincidence?"

A shrug. "Could be."

So that was how he was going to play it. The Old Man had already sniffed out where this was headed and didn't like it.

Two years ago – July 9, 1936, to be exact – we get this telegram from England. Sir Edgar Parker-Davies of London wanted to hire an American gumshoe to regain a stolen artifact. In some roundabout way – via a niece or something who lived in San Francisco and knew somebody who'd had success with the agency – he'd heard good things about my work and wanted to hire me at triple the daily rate. The Old man and I thought it was some kind of joke at first. London had Scotland Yard and more than its share of private dicks. But he telegraphed the details back to the limey and the next day Sir Edgar wired us the money, prepaying for thirty days of my time, plus travel expenses.

The Old Man, of course, was delighted.

I jumped a rattler to New York and then sailed to London. I remember fantasizing at the time about taking a zeppelin across, but Sir Edgar's travel allowance wouldn't cover the cost of that. Too bad. The *Hindenburg* blow the following year canceled all zeppelin traffic, so I missed my chance for good. A long trip, and all the time I was wondering why an American detective? And of all American detectives, why me?

When I finally met Sir Edgar, all walrus mustache and funny accent, in his overstuffed apartment, he offered a number of reasons. The first was my success rate. He'd checked up on me and found that only rarely did I fail to deliver. But so what? I told him I was sure plenty of limey private gumshoes had similar clearance rates. He agreed, but none of them had wanted to take on this case because it involved some mysterious chink in the Limehouse district, a guy with no known name but referred to by the coolies as the Lord of Strange Deaths. And Sir Edgar couldn't go to the police because the artifact didn't legally belong to him. Seemed he'd lifted it off someone when he and his fellow Brits left Shanghai earlier in the year as hostilities heated up between the chinks and the Japs.

What was this precious artifact?

He showed me a photo he'd made: a small, stoppered jar of nephritic jade, carved into the shape of a dragon claw. Valuable in and of itself for the workmanship, but priceless because of what it contained: powdered dragon tongue.

I couldn't help it. I laughed in his face.

It didn't bother him. He seemed to be expecting it. He told me he'd come to appreciate the ancient ways of China while stationed there with the diplomatic corps. He said – pointedly – that most westerners were ignorant of Oriental cultures and therefore couldn't appreciate them.

Yeah, but powdered dragon tongue?

I said I didn't have to appreciate anything. If he wanted his little jade jar back, I'd do my best to find it for him. All he had to do was point me toward this Limehouse place and I'd get started.

But no, I wouldn't be going to Limehouse, I'd be sailing back to New York. He'd learned through a source in the Chinese Embassy that word on the streets of Limehouse was that the Lord of Strange Deaths had departed for America – for New York, to be specific. If Sir Edgar had been able to notify me before setting sail, he would have, but he'd learned only two days ago.

Frankly, I was relieved. The agency had a New York office – we didn't call ourselves Continental for nothing – with lots of contacts, and I'd be lots more at home dealing with American cops than London bobbies.

I headed back on the next ship out. But when I docked and checked in with the New York office, I learned that Sir Edgar was dead and I should return to San Francisco. But I didn't go right away. I did a little sniffing around and turned up a shady chink known as Shiwan Khan. I thought he might be a new identity taken on by the lord of strange deaths, but no. Talking to some local coolies I gathered this guy was something of an amateur compared to the one I was seeking. Besides, he'd run up against some kook in a cape and a slouch hat and hadn't come out so well.

So I trained back and tried to forgot about Sir Edgar and his powdered dragon tongue. Did a pretty good job until today.

"Why this trip down memory lane?" the Old Man said.

"You know Hank Sorenson?"

"The flatfoot on the Chinatown Squad? Heard he was sick."

"So did I. Figured it's the flu or something like that. Then I'm having coffee with a Potrero door shaker and he tells me Sorenson's sick from the bite of a giant millipede found only in the jungles of Borneo or someplace like that."

"So?"

Still playing dumb.

"So Sorenson almost died – might still die. And wouldn't you call that a *strange death*?"

The Old Man made a sour face. "I see where you're going, but Borneo's a long way from Africa where the limey's puff adder came from."

"Yeah, but they both ended up a long, long ways from where they started. Word is Sorenson was trying to put the bite on a mysterious chink bigshot on his beat when something put the bite on him."

"Let me guess: This Chinatown bigshot is known to the locals as the Lord Of Strange Deaths."

"As a matter of fact, no. He's known as the Mandarin."

"Well, there you go. Now–"

"I'm gonna take a couple of days to look into it."

"Not on the agency's time, you're not."

"Yeah, I am. By my calculation, we still owe the limey about ten days."

The Old man reddened – he wasn't liking this at all. "What in blazes are you talking about?"

"Sir Edgar prepaid thirty. I spent eight days getting there, eight days getting back, and wasted four more in Manhattan on that Shiwan Kahn dead end. That leaves ten still in the till."

"He's not a client anymore. He's dead. Case closed. And more important, *account* closed."

"No," I said, shaking my head. "Not closed. Not by a long shot. Don't buck me on this. I won't be spending ten days on it – nothing near that. But whatever time I do spend has already been paid for. So where's your beef? We owe it to the guy."

The Old Man tapped his pencil on the desk as he stared at me. "'We owe it to the guy.' Don't come at me with that. Who do you think you're kidding? I've seen you pad expenses with the best of them." He leaned forward. "The client's dead. It's off our books. It's a closed case."

"Not for me."

"That's it, isn't it. This isn't about the limey, it's about you. What do you do – keep a private score?"

I rose from the chair and headed for the door. "I'll file reports as usual."

"See that you do."

A private score…the old bastard had hit the bull's eye on that one. I'd never got close to the Lord of Strange Deaths – not even within shouting distance – and it had been eating at my gut for two years. This might all lead to nothing. If so, so be it. But if this Mandarin character and the Lord of Strange Deaths were the same lug, I wanted to know. And then there was the matter of a little jade jar…

*

I got hold of Detective Sergeant Hank Sorenson's phone number through the Chinatown Squad's station house and called him. We go back a little. I said I'd buy him lunch in exchange for a little talk. He was fine with that, then rattled a harsh laugh and added, "Long as it ain't Chinese."

So we arranged to meet for Guinea food at Luigi's on Columbus Avenue in North Beach. On the way over the fog lifted enough for a glimpse of the Coit Tower on Telegraph Hill. Hard to believe it had been there five years already.

In walked into Luigi's and got slammed with a shock. Hank Sorenson looked like death warmed over. And not very well warmed over at that: sunken cheeks, deeper sunken eyes, skin the color of dumpling dough. The cop must have lost fifty pounds since I'd last seen him.

I acted like everything was okay and ordered the veal rollatini. Sorenson chose the linguini and white clam sauce.

After the waiter was gone, Sorenson gestured around at the restaurant. "What's this all about? You thinking of placing a bet so you're checking me out?"

I looked at him. "Bet on what?"

"Don't tell me you don't know."

"Haven't the faintest. Been out of town." And that was the truth.

"Then why the lunch?"

"I heard you had a run-in with a lug I might be interested in."

"Yeah?"

"The Mandarin."

He was reaching for the bread and his hand froze halfway there. It started to shake, and the shake traveled up his arm and passed through his body as a head-to-toe shudder.

"Let's talk about something else," he said in a whisper.

"Just a few questions."

"He'll hear about it. He'll know what we say." His gaze darted right, then left. "He has eyes and ears everywhere."

I doubted that. Maybe in Chinatown. This was Little Italy.

"He's why I'm like this," he added.

"I heard about the millipede. The poison do this to you?"

"Poison?" He barked that same rattle-laugh I'd heard on the phone. "If only!" He pulled back a sleeve, revealing a skeletal arm, and checked his watch. "Which reminds me."

He pulled out a cigarette case, opened it, and removed what looked like a red cigarette, but the paper was twisted closed at both ends. He held it up to his mouth with both hands, snapped it open, and inhaled the fine gray powder within.

Had the bite turned him into some sort of hop head?

"What's that?" I said.

He crumpled the paper and dropped it in the ashtray. "Medicine."

Sight of his cigarette case started a nicotine itch. I pulled out a pack of Luckies and lit one. I offered but he shook his head. I set the pack on the table and the lighter atop it.

"Nice lighter," he said.

Its brass finish fit pretty well with the green of the Lucky Strike pack.

"Something new under the sun," I said. "It's called a Zippo. Supposed to be windproof but I haven't tested that yet." Since he didn't want to talk about his condition, I got down to the reason for meeting him. "Tell me what you know about the Mandarin."

"Tell me what *you* know and I'll see if I have anything to add."

"All I know is that he runs all the crime and vices in Coolietown."

"Right there, you're wrong. He doesn't run anything. He lets the tongs and triads run the games and the whores and the opium and the protection rackets. He simply sits back and takes a cut."

"Must be nice. How does one get in that position?"

"Anyone who bucks him dies...horribly."

"What you might call 'strange deaths'?"

Sorenson nodded. "*Very* strange."

This was sounding better and better. I could foresee one problem, though.

"Been here forever, I imagine."

"As a matter of fact, no one had heard of him until about two years ago when he blew into town and took over."

Just what I wanted to hear.

We waited while the waiter served our meals. The veal smelled great, but it could wait. As soon as we were alone again, I leaned forward.

"This Mandarin lug. What's he look like?"

Sorenson poked at his linguine. The clams were lined up along the rim of the plate, shells gaping.

"Never saw him."

That didn't fit. "But I heard–"

"That I was trying to shake him down? Believe what you like, but I never laid eyes on him. And people who have ain't talking about it. Except one, maybe."

He had my interest now. "Who?"

His reply was interrupted by a coughing fit, deep wracking hacks that got the attention of the other lunchers in the place. At least it got come color into his face. After one especially deep hack that seemed to originate in his bunions, something popped out of his mouth and landed on the linguine. It was the same color as his clams but was about an inch long, and thin. I looked closer and noticed it was rimmed with what looked like legs.

I leaned back. "Oh, hell!"

Sorenson wasn't fazed in the least. In fact, he picked up his butter knife and poked at it.

"It's dead," he whispered. "Dear God, it's dead!"

"Let's hope so," I said.

He looked up at me, eyes bright, his face showing the first sign of animation since he'd walked in.

"Don't you see what this means? It's dead – that means I'm winning!"

"You mean before this you've been coughing up live ones?"

He nodded excitedly. "Yes!"

He tossed the dead worm or baby millipede or whatever it was on the floor and dug into his linguine. I looked at my veal and realized I'd lost my appetite. I'm no sensitive houseplant. I've pulled triggers, I've put holes in people – had a hole or two drilled through me as well – and seen my share of blood and guts. But nothing like this. Give me mayhem anytime.

"Take mine home for later. I've got to run. I'll take care of the bill on my way out. Just give me the name of the fellow who saw him."

"A green soft-heel named Brannigan," Sorenson said. "You probably read about him in the *Chronicle* – that ship that blew up?"

Oh, I knew all about Brannigan. "The cop who saved the girls?"

"That's the one. He was in the same room as the Mandarin that night."

Then he was the one I needed to talk to.

"Thanks," I said, rising and going in search of Luigi to settle up. He'd be upset I was leaving my food, but no way around it.

I knew I'd be seeing that worm in my dreams.

*

Everybody in town knew about Detective Brad Brannigan – hard not to after he'd been plastered all over the front of the Chronicle last week: hero of the waterfront, risking his skin to save all those gals from lives of slavery.

That should have been me. Or at least us. He could have shared what he knew.

But I'm not one to hold a grudge, especially since I probably would have held out on him if places had been reversed. Earned himself a promotion from detective three to detective two. From what I'd read, it sounded like he deserved it.

I had a nodding acquaintance with Hanrahan, Brannigan's chief. He told me this was the kid's day off but gave me his home address in Eureka Valley. No surprise there: an Irish cop in an Irish working-class area.

The fog hadn't seeped that far inland, so the sun sat high and bright above Castro Street where I found him in the shade alongside the big Victorian house where he rented an apartment. He had thick dark hair, bright blue eyes, and was busy waxing a brand new shark-nosed Graham. I'd seen pictures of the Graham in the papers but this was my first look in real life. Its model name was "Spirit of Motion." A man could fall in love with a car like that. I mean, in real love.

A freshly minted detective second grade with a shiny new shark-nose meant one thing: He was on the pad.

I reintroduced myself.

"Yeah, I remember," he said. "You looking for another gone gal?"

I shook my head. "This is something different. I was talking to Sorenson and he said I should see you."

"How's he doing?" he asked.

"Looks like one foot in the grave and the other on a banana peel, but seems to think he's getting better."

"Well, I hope he makes it. And I hope he learned his lesson."

I knew what Brannigan meant, but couldn't believe he was saying that while he waxed a newly minted Graham.

"How much do these things run?" I asked, hoping he got the point.

He shrugged. "Don't know. It was a gift."

"Must be nice to have a rich uncle."

He gave me a hard look. "It arrived two nights ago. Fully paid for, with all the paperwork. No mention of who from."

"You must have an idea."

"Oh, yeah, I got an idea, all right. Somebody very grateful he got his daughter back in one piece. But I don't know his name, so I can't give it back."

"He's gonna want something in return. It's known as *quid pro quo*." At least that's what the Old Man calls it.

"Not this guy."

He seemed pretty sure of that.

"So you figure you might as well enjoy it." Just what I'd do.

"Damn right. What can I do for you?"

"Hunting a big-shot chink crook. The trail started in London, dried up in New York, but now I think he landed here."

He stopped polishing. "The Mandarin?"

"Could be."

"Well, unless this is really – and I mean, *really* personal, your life will be simpler and last lots longer if you leave it alone."

"It's personal enough. Sorenson says you've seen this coolie. Care to give me a description?"

Brannigan resumed polishing. "Tell you what: You give *me* the description of the guy you're after and I'll tell you if they're the same."

"Never laid eyes on him."

"Then how–?"

"We may be talking about different people altogether, but I want to know this mugg when I see him."

"You won't see him. But if you happen across a tall, skinny Chinaman with a high forehead, thinning hair, and – get this – green eyes, you've found him."

"Green eyes? Never seen a chink with green eyes."

"Pray you don't see his. Because they might be the last thing you ever see."

"You saw them and you look pretty healthy to me."

"Only by luck. Only because the guy who sent me this car was there. Those eyes…" He gave his shoulders a quick roll, like he was shaking off a chill. "They look right through you. It's like they read your soul." Another shoulder roll.

Before he could get all Garbo on me, I said, "When you were there, did you happen to see a little jade jar carved like a dragon's claw?"

"If something like that was there, I missed it. I was kind of busy staying alive."

Fair enough.

"One last question: Where do I find him?"

He shook his head. "You don't want to."

"Oh, but I do."

He looked me straight in the eyes. "So did Sorenson, and look where it got him."

I wasn't going to end up like Sorenson. And I wasn't about to let a green cop give me the willies.

"Come on. My clock's running. Where'd you see him?"

Brannigan hesitated, then said, "The Yan Yuap Tong house. It's on–"

"I know where it is."

"But–"

I waved as I turned away. "Thanks."

At least I had a starting point.

*

I waited for dark and then headed for Chinatown, a coolie-packed square mile or so in the heart of downtown. The fog had thickened to cotton and coated every surface with beads of water. Wet enough to warrant a raincoat, which I'd worn – for multiple reasons. I found a darkened doorway off Stockton Street with a view of the headquarters of the Yan Yuap – Dragon – Tong, and eased back into its shadows. The fog had eaten the tong house's cupola'd roof, but lanterns and a window or two glowed here and there within its black bulk.

Like the other San Francisco tongs these days, the Dragons tried to keep up a legit front while seeking to maintain the level of influence it had over the local vices during the Tong Wars of the 1880s and 90s. All that changed in 1906 when the earthquake and fire razed Chinatown – where everything had been built of tinder wood – to the pavement and below. The tongs never recovered their former glory, but still wielded considerable power over daily life down here.

The aught-six quake and fire were sort of like the Great Flood in the Bible: All public records disappeared along with the buildings. Everything had to start again from scratch. Including my life.

I survived the disaster, but I don't remember a thing about it. I was only two at the time and was found wandering the waterfront, scorched but otherwise unhurt. I couldn't tell anyone my name or where I lived. I have no memory of my home or my folks, and have to assume they didn't survive. Like the city, I started again from zero, and my life after that was a series of foster homes, the less said about, the better.

I lit a cigarette. I wasn't worried about the smoke or the glowing tip giving me away. Anyone who cared knew where I was. Chinatown was quiet tonight, and this little side street even quieter. The immigration laws had restricted the number of chinks allowed into the country and the population had dwindled. I was thinking of making a casual circuit around the tong house when I heard the slap of slippers approaching along the sidewalk. I pressed back, waiting for whoever it was to pass. But the footsteps stopped.

I looked around and saw a Chinese gal staring up at me. She wore a hooded cloak of dark cloth that ran down to her ankles. The light was dim but I could see she had one of those Oriental faces that are so hard to date – she could have been thirty, could have been fifty. Black eyes peered at me through thick, horn-rimmed glasses. She sure as hell wasn't a dolla-dolla girl looking for some trade.

"What do you want?" I said.

She sing-songed her reply through a heavy accent. Her voice was soft but the words hit like a hard-knuckled punch.

"You seek Mandarin? You no find him here."

I stared at her in mute shock for a second of two. How the hell could she know that? I shook it off and said, "I'm not looking for anyone. Just killing time. Move along."

Her black eyes looked me up and down appraisingly. "I know where he is."

I bit back a laugh. "And you're gonna tell me – just like that?"

She shook her head. "Not here."

I eased my right hand into the pocket of my raincoat. I'd brought my .38. It didn't take much imagination to see how this was planned to go: She'd lure me into a building or an alley where some of the Mandarin's highbinder hatchet men would reduce me to a bloody jigsaw puzzle and leave the pieces for the coroner to reassemble.

"Where then?"

"You buy me nice dinner and maybe I tell you."

"'Maybe'?"

"Must see if you are worthy."

I hadn't expected that. Rather than get into her definition of worthy, I remained wary. A little hole-in-the-wall restaurant could serve as a killing floor just as well as an alley. I played along.

"I don't know the neighborhood. Where do you suggest?"

She made a face. "Not here! You take me nice restaurant. I want American food."

Another surprise.

"You like steak?"

She smiled, and I had to admit she had a lovely smile. Dazzling, in fact. She told me she loved sirloin, but with her accent it came out "ruv siroin."

John's Grill down near Market Street on Ellis was less than a mile from where we stood but a whole universe away from Chinatown.

"You're on," I said.

I stepped out of the doorway and down to the sidewalk. She was taller than my first impression. We began the short walk over to Powell where we could catch the cable car down to Ellis. As was the gentlemanly custom, I took the curbside, to protect the woman from splashes from the street – and to place her between me and whoever might jump from a doorway.

Along the way I kept a tight grip on the .38 in my pocket.

*

John's Grill was one of the first places to open after the fire. It boasted dark oak paneling and damask tablecloths. The conversation level dropped and I caught a slew of dirty looks from the bar area when I walked in with a chinky-girl. The maitre d' acted like we were invisible even though I saw a fair number of empty tables scattered around the floor.

"You will take my wrap?" she said.

Wrap. Listen to this one.

"Maybe you oughta keep it on. We may not get seated."

"Oh, we get seat."

She turned, flipped back the hood, and shrugged out of the cape. I caught it and folded it over an arm – not for long, I figured. We'd be back on the street real soon.

Then she turned around.

If the conversation level had dropped when we stepped in, it fell off a cliff now. She had raven black hair cut in a bob and her slim body was wrapped in a slinky, high-collared, red silk sheath decorated with golden dragons that coiled from her shoulders to her ankles.

I turned when I heard the maitre d' clear his throat behind me.

"We can offer you a window table or a corner booth, sir. Which would you prefer?"

"Booth," I said, sounding a tad hoarse. "Definitely a booth."

*

Well, her name was Nuying and she did indeed ruv siroin.

I watched her slim ivory hands slice off delicate bloody rare slices and slide them between her ruby lips. Now that she'd shed the hooded cloak and the light was better, I noticed how pale she was – just a hint of yellow to her skin. She'd removed her thick lenses to eat and her eyes looked wider than the average Oriental's. This gal was some sort of Eurasian.

After flirting with the idea of a Dungeness platter, I'd settled on a big porterhouse, but I kept finding myself looking at her. She was stunning. But I wasn't about to let that distract me.

"So," I said, drawing out the word, "where do I find the Mandarin?"

She put down her knife and fork and lifted her wine glass. She'd ordered a Californian red –

Californian! Nobody drank California wine, even before they'd been shut down by prohibition. Prohibition had been given the boot only five years ago. I'd noticed the label said *Inglenook*. Whoever heard of naming a wine Inglenook? Me, I always ate a steak with bourbon and a splash.

She sipped her wine and leaned forward. Her pale cheeks were flushed. Maybe she wasn't used to wine. I'd heard Orientals and booze don't mix well.

"You do not find him standing outside Yan Yuap tong house, silly man."

"He was seen there."

"Do you know *anything* of Chinatown?"

"A fair amount."

"Have you ever cut open anthill? Chinatown like anthill. You have many building above, many, many passage below. If *boo hoo dow doy* want, he enter joss house on Pine Street and come out restaurant on Broadway."

"I thought all those secret passages were destroyed in the earthquake."

"Can rebuild what destroyed." She waggled a slim, ivory-hued finger at me. "Round eyes never catch Chinaman in Chinatown. Not without help."

"And you're going to help me?"

"First you tell me why you want Mandarin."

I wanted to be asking the questions. I watched the pupils of her black eyes closely as I said, "Ever hear of the Lord of Strange Deaths?"

No change. She merely shrugged and said, "Of course."

"He disappeared from London a couple of years ago; this Mandarin character showed up here about the same time. I'm wondering if they're to the same. You have any thoughts on that?"

A sip, a shrug. "I only his concubine."

I damn near dropped my fork. "His concu – then you must know–"

She shook her head. "I with him only one year."

I leaned back and gave her a hard stare. This stank of a setup like the wharves in August. But as long as I had her here…

"First things first: How did you know I was looking for the Mandarin?"

Another shrug, another sip. "I overhear Jiang Zhifu tell him man asking cops about Mandarin." Before I could ask how he could know, she said, "Mandarin keep eye and ear on Detective Sorenson."

I could imagine why: waiting for the millipede bite to take its ultimate toll. And I'd gone and had a public conversation with Sorenson. Well, even a private talk might have been overheard.

"You're his concubine, you say. That's some sort of sex slave, isn't it?"

"Sex?" Her laugh was musical. I know people call laughs musical, but this one had a genuine tinklely sound to it. "He not touch Nuying. Ever. He only look."

I wasn't following. "You mean he watches you have sex with someone else?"

That laugh again. "Silly man. He not interest sex. I pose. He look."

These Orientals were strange-strange-strange. "Pose how?"

"After dinner, we go your place. I show."

Was that it? She'd been sent to find where I live?

"It's a long way from here," I told her.

She frowned. "No, it not. It on Ivy Street."

I squeezed the handle of my steak knife. "How do you know that?"

"Jiang Zhifu tell master."

All right. Enough of this.

"And I'm supposed to believe the Mandarin just lets his concubine out to wander the streets and pick up gumshoes for a meal?"

"He leave town two day. I bored. I tired dim sum. Like steak. Like wine. You eat. We go. I show you pose."

*

Maybe it was her laugh. Maybe it was the whiskey. Whatever the reason, we wound up at my place. And we were both a little tipsy, she more than I. After all, she was a slip of a thing and she'd downed that whole bottle of wine.

After I hung up her cloak I went to the cabinet where I keep a bottle of Beam.

"I don't have wine," I told her. "But I do have–"

I turned and froze. All her clothing lay in a pile on the floor. The stood there in her birthday suit, balancing on her left foot, her right arm and leg stretched behind her, her left arm pointing ahead. She had small sleek breasts, and not a hair on her body.

"This what I do for Master."

I couldn't speak. With her white skin she looked like a statue – literally. For she posed statue still. Not a waver, not a tremor, despite the awkward pose.

She said, "Then he point and I move."

In a fluid motion she assumed a new stance, equally graceful.

"Sometime I hold hours."

My gaze traveled the lines of her alabaster body. She was…exquisite.

"I taught thousand way to please man-flesh, yet this all Master want." She dropped the pose and glided toward me. She placed her hands against my chest. "I need show man what I know. You be that man?"

I still couldn't speak. But I could nod.

*

In my business you deal in facts.

Fact: I am thick and on the short side, not the sort women gravitate to.

Fact: She was not attracted to me.

Fact: She'd had a lot to drink and needed a man.

Fact: I was handy.

Fact: I have never experienced anything like that night before or since.

A thousand ways to please man-flesh…

She needed only a few to leave me weak and exhausted.

I awoke at sunup because I always awaken at sunup. I was facing the wall. I remembered last night and at first thought it had been one hell of a dream. And then I heard her sobbing.

I rolled over and found her sitting on the edge of the bed, her bare back to me.

"What's wrong?"

"I will be punished," she said without turning. "Staff tell Master when he return."

I didn't like the sound of that. Not one bit.

"Punished how?"

"He have many way – way that leave no mark."

No, he wouldn't want to mar that perfect skin.

"Then don't go back."

"I must. If Master have to look for Nuying, he punish worse." She glanced at me over her shoulder. "No can stay here. He know about you."

As enticing as it was to think that every night could be like last night, I hadn't been considering an invitation. I was glad she'd taken it off the table.

"Can you get out of town?"

She shook her head. "I have no money."

"Neither do I," I said quickly.

I felt like an overwound spring. I couldn't get a bead on this whole situation. I'd spent the night with a beautiful expert in the sexual arts. I'm no patsy. I've investigated too many cons and hustles to know that a thing that seems too good to be true usually is. I'd been around too long to believe this was just what it appeared to be. So what was it? A shakedown? A trap? When would I find some hideous poisonous *thing* in my bed?

Then, in a barely audible voice, she said, "I know where Master keep money," and everything fell into place.

I let out a sigh of relief and felt my tight muscles relax. *Quid pro quo*. That I understood. I'd enjoyed the *quid*. Now I'd be expected to provide the *quo*.

I decided to play along. "Where would that be?"

"In wall behind hanging. He think I not know, but I see. He keep key all time." She sniffed and gave me another teary look over her shoulder. "You know how open lock?"

"Oh, yeah. I can pick a lock with the best of them. How much money we talking here?"

She turned. Her small brown nipples jutted toward me. "No dolla bill. Gold and jewel."

A little chime sounded in my brain. A place where the Mandarin stored his valuables. Might those valuable include...?

"Jade too?"

She shrugged. "Jade, yes. Much jade, but jade not worth like gold and diamond."

A certain piece was "worth" to me.

I lifted the covers. "Get back under here and we'll figure a way to get you into your masters hidey hole. But first..."

Now that I knew how to supply the *quo*, I figured I deserved a little more *quid*.

*

I like to keep things simple, and the plan we cooked up fit the bill.

The Mandarin was scheduled to return tomorrow. Nuying knew only that he and his minion Jiang Zhifu had gone off to finalize a purchase from someone she'd heard mentioned as "Oliver." She didn't know when he'd return tomorrow, so that gave us today.

After my second helping of *quid* I was – I admit it – weak-kneed until I'd had some coffee and eggs. I ate alone as Nuying returned to the Mandarin's place. She'd given me the address – a place on Stone Street, near the Chinese Hospital on Jackson. I was to meet her there at 12:30 sharp.

I headed for the agency. I said hello to Effie as she stepped out of the Spade & Archer office down the hall from ours, but she barely acknowledged my existence. I was used to that. Discretion being the better part of valor, I avoided the Old Man. He'd be asking questions and wouldn't like the answers.

I closed myself off in a cubicle and practiced with my rakes and tension bars. They say lock picking is like riding a bike, and in a way it is – once you've gotten used to feeling those pins fall into place and the cylinder turn, you can always go back to it. But I hadn't done it for a while and I wanted a little honing. I wanted to get in and out of the Mandarin's lair as quickly as possible.

Nuying had no idea what kind of lock it was, so I had to be ready for anything. She'd said it had a key, so that was the important thing. A combination lock was beyond me.

At 12:30 sharp I knocked on the front door of a very ordinary brick building. Nuying, wearing a black tunic and loose black pants, let me in. She carried a drawstring purse and her expression was strained.

"Must hurry. Master change plan – come home today."

"Today?" I didn't like that. This was supposed to be a simple snatch and run. "Why didn't you tell me?"

"How?"

Good question. She had no way of reaching me. Even if she'd had my home number, I hadn't been there all day.

"Move!" I said. We had to squeeze the minutes.

She led me through a succession of plainly furnished rooms – Oriental furniture, to be sure, but nothing fancy – toward the rear of the house. Not at all what I'd expected for the overlord of Chinatown crime. And where were his minions?

"Aren't there any–?" I began as we passed the kitchen.

Half a dozen people lay sprawled on the floor or slumped across a food-littered table.

"I drug tea," she said. "They sleep hours."

That answered that question, but I still wondered…

"I expected more lavish surroundings."

"Master not care for comfort."

I knew the type. Power fueled their engine. This Mandarin was skimming ten percent of Chinatown's vice take and sitting on secondhand furniture. The money didn't go on his walls or on his back or into his belly. It bought influence in high places. Power.

But I still didn't know if the coolie who lived here and the Lord of Strange Deaths were one and the same. I hoped his treasure cabinet held the answer. Then I'd be settled straight with the late Sir Edgar and could send Nuying on her way to a place where she'd never have to pose naked for some yellow pervert again.

She led me upstairs to a second-floor room where all four walls were hung with elaborate Oriental rugs. At last, a show of extravagance. I noticed a brown-skinned figure lying facedown in a corner. I'd expected the place to be guarded by hatchet-wielding, black-pajama'd *boo hoo dow doys*. This one wore only a white loincloth.

"Who's that?"

"One of Master's dacoits. Come all way from Burma. He sleep now."

The wall rugs covered the windows so the room was lit by electric sconces between the hangings. A curved chair with a high back sat on a low dais against the wall.

"This where Master hold meeting," Nuying said.

"Where's this cabinet?"

She grabbed the edge of one of the hangings and pulled. It slid sideways on a track to reveal a steel door set in the wall. The cabinet itself was no doubt bolted to the support beams in the wall. An ornate red-and-yellow lacquered dragon had been carved into the steel. What was it with these coolies and dragons? No knob or handle on the door, just an indented groove for fingertips. And just above the groove: the lock.

I didn't see the name of the maker or locksmith anywhere. No matter. I knew the lock had to be fairly new. This particular building was maybe fifteen years old – somebody had learned a lesson from the quake and fire and built it with brick – and so the safe couldn't be any older.

I went to work with Nuying pacing behind me, wringing her empty purse in her delicate hands.

"Nervous?" I said as I inserted a tension bar into the keyhole.

"Yes. If Master catch me…" She didn't need to finish.

"I'll see that he doesn't."

The pins didn't respond to the first two rakes, but the third began getting results.

"Almost there."

"I hear car," she said.

I glanced over my shoulder as she moved to one of the drapes on the far side of the room. She lifted it a few inches and peeked out.

"Not for this building," she said.

"Keep watch. I'll just be–"

I felt the last pin drop and the cylinder rotate a couple of degrees.

A little voice was sounding in the back of my brain, saying this was too easy. Well, it was, and it wasn't. I had inside help, otherwise I wouldn't have known of the cabinet or even the house. The place had been guarded but again, my inside help had doped all the troops.

I dropped the rake and slipped my fingertips into the groove. The bolt inside was heavy and I didn't want the short end of my tension rod breaking off in the keyhole. *No one* would be able to open it then. The door had minimal give but I wiggled it best I could as I levered the little rod. The cylinder turned slowly, slowly, until the bolt suddenly snapped back. The door must have been perfectly balanced on its hinges because it swung open with an ease that took me by surprise. I stumbled back–

–and good thing too.

Something hissed and a long, olive-colored snake shot from the cabinet. I had a glimpse of the black insides of its open mouth, its extended fangs. Nuying screamed and did a little dance as it wriggled its eight-foot body across the floor and disappeared behind the lower end of one of the hangings.

"You didn't tell me there was a snake in there!"

"Never was!" she cried, eyes wide. "Master must put when leave!"

Looking at the inside of the door now I saw air holes, camouflaged by the dragon carved into the outer surface.

Well, I'd thought it was too easy. The snake changed my mind. I'd done a little research on the things after Sir Edgar's death. By all the descriptions I'd read, that was a black mamba – the black referring not to its skin color but the inside of its mouth. Deadliest snake in Africa when provoked, but shy by nature. It would stay put behind that rug as long as we didn't bother it. And we weren't going to do that.

"Hai!" Nuying looked stricken as she approached the open cabinet. "Where gold? Where jewel?"

I saw what she meant. Only a few gold objects on the shelf, looking lost and lonely. But I noticed something green off to the side and caught my breath when I recognized Sir Edgar's dragon-claw jar. I grabbed it and worked the tight stopper free. Gray powder, like ash, filled the inside. Powdered dragon tongue. Sure, if you believed that, I had a big, rust-colored bridge I could sell you.

As I restoppered the bottle, Nuying said, "What you have? That not worth. How I am escape?"

"This is for me. You can have the rest."

"Not enough!" She looked ready to cry as she loosened the drawstrings on her purse.

I began sweeping anything that looked valuable off the shelves and stuffing it into the purse.

"It'll get you a start."

I knew a jeweler who'd give her a good price on my say-so and have the gold melted down and the stones reset before I put her on a train out of town.

A car door slammed outside. This time I heard it too. Keeping my distance from the spot where I'd last seen the snake, I hurried across the room and lifted one of the drapes. A black-robed coolie was opening the rear door of a sedan. A taller chink with a skullcap and thinning hair got out. I ducked back and tripped over the prone dacoit. My hand touched his back. Cold. He felt…dead.

I threw Nuying a questioning look but her features had gone slack with terror.

"Him?" she whispered.

"I'm assuming yes. There a back way out?"

She didn't say anything, she simply ran. I followed her downstairs to the ground floor, past the kitchen littered with still forms. Were they dead too? Had she miscalculated the dose of whatever drug she'd used and overdosed them all?

I'd worry about that later. Down another set of steps to a damp cellar. She tore aside a tapestry to reveal a door in the wall. She pulled it open and hesitated. Darkness awaited.

"Where's this take us?"

"Many places."

The famous Chinatown underground. We didn't have time to wait, and anyplace was better than here.

Somebody had to take the lead, so I ducked past her. I didn't have a flashlight but I had my Zippo. I hoped it was windproof like they said because I intended to be moving as fast as I could. When Nuying closed the door behind us, I lost all bearings. I spun the wheel on the lighter and a flame appeared. I held it straight out before me and started moving. It threw little light but was better than nothing.

We'd gone about twenty feet when something sharp pricked the back of my neck. I slapped at the spot but found nothing. Had something bitten me?

Ten paces or so later, my legs began to feel wobbly. Another three or four and they gave out. I landed on my knees and pitched forward. I was able to break my fall with my arms, but an instant later they were useless. The Zippo skittered away ahead of me.

"Nuying?"

I felt a hand in my jacket pocket. Sir Edgar's jade – I tried to stop her but I couldn't even speak now. She wrestled the jar free. Something dropped by my face; metal clinked within – her purse with the gold. Didn't she want it?

I saw her pick up the lighter and hurry away down the black passage. The faint glow became fainter.

I heard a high-pitched yelp of either shock or terror, and then the darkness became complete.

*

The first thing I became aware of was the rocking. Next was the cold steel floor against my cheek. I lifted my aching head and opened my eyes. Details slowly registered as my vision cleared: a single bulb swaying on a cord overhead, oblong wooden crates stacked on all sides, Nuying sitting crosslegged on the floor a dozen feet away.

"You!" I said, fighting nausea and vertigo as I pushed myself halfway up to a sitting position.

She stared through me, saying nothing, not even acknowledging my presence. And as she stared I noticed something: Her eyes were green now.

I felt something around my neck – a steel collar, with a chain running to a ring in the floor. I noticed a similar collar encircling Nuying's throat.

"Where are we?"

Again, no response.

I weathered more vertigo as I struggled to my feet. When the world steadied again, I looked around. I had enough chain to stand and that was it. Not enough to reach Nuying. If it had allowed that, I might have strangled her.

Obviously we were in the hold of some sort of cargo ship. The sway of the floor and the vibrations running through it told me we were underway. But what was the cargo?

A stack of the crates sat close behind me. I examined the nearest in the dim light. They were nailed shut but I could read the stenciling along the top.

Springfield Armory
M1903

Add that to the length of the crates and these had to be Springfield M1903 rifles. I looked around at all the crates – there had to be hundreds, no, thousands of them in the hold.

I turned to Nuying. "What's going on here?"

Again, nothing.

"What did you do to me?"

"She poisoned you and betrayed you," said a soft voice from above.

I looked up and saw a tall, thin, high-shouldered Chinaman in a floor-length robe of embroidered yellow silk standing on an overhead gangway. Thin black hair flowed from under a brimless beaded cap. Beneath that, a high, domed forehead arched to a pair of light green eyes. The eyes identified him: the criminal overlord known as the Mandarin.

And because of the contents of his cabinet, I now knew he was also called the Lord of Strange Deaths.

He turned his emerald gaze on Nuying. "You are expert at that, are you not, Fah lo Suee?" He hissed the "s" softly.

I turned to her as well. "Is that your real name? I guess I shouldn't be surprised."

Still, she didn't react.

The Mandarin said, "She has gone by many names: Madame Ingomar, Queen Mamaloi, Ling Moy, Lin Tang. What was it this time, my dear?"

Since she wasn't speaking, I answered for her. "Nuying. I suppose because that's easier to pronounce than Fah lo Suee."

"Oh, she would never use 'Fah lo Suee.' That is merely a term of endearment for my daughter."

I felt as if I'd been punched. But looking at her eyes now, I couldn't deny the truth.

"Daughter! She said she was your concubine!"

A soft laugh. "Did she now? Such an imagination."

"But her eyes were black!"

"Scleral lenses. Not terribly new. Usually used to improve vision, but tinted ones can change eye color." He smiled. "Did she adequately demonstrate to you the talents of a skilled concubine?"

Now was my turn to keep silent. This gal had played me like a maestro. She'd softened me up with sex and told me just enough of what I wanted to hear and then let me fill in the blanks the way I wanted them filled.

Finally, when I could look at her again, I said, "Why?" I gestured around at the crates. "Was it all about these?"

"All about them and nothing about them," the Mandarin said. "Isn't that right, Fah lo Suee?"

Still she refused to speak or even look at her father.

"This model is being replaced by a newer design, so a man who was once an enemy got me 'a good deal,' as you people say."

"What are you going to do?" I said to him. "Start a war?"

"End one, I hope. As for my daughter's scheme, I have a good idea as to her purpose, but I shall let her tell us herself."

Now she reacted, leaping to her feet and crying, "No! Not that!"

He clapped his hands once and said, "Jiang Zhifu will do the honors."

The daughter's voice rose to a scream. "*NO!*"

Was he going to torture her? His own daughter?

A black-pajama'd chink appeared from nowhere carrying not instruments of torture but a small jade jar shaped like a dragon's claw.

"Sir Edgar's!" I said.

"No," said the Mandarin. "Mine."

The one called Jiang Zhifu placed the jar on one of the crates and removed the top. He dipped his finger in the powder and then approached the daughter – I didn't know what to call her. She whimpered and cringed away, straining against the chain that bound her to the floor.

She wailed as Jiang Zhifu pounced on her like a cat, yanked her head back, and rubbed his finger inside her cheek. He released her and immediately she began spitting out whatever he'd dosed her with. He paid her no mind as he returned to the jade jar, stoppered it, and faded again into the shadows.

"Powdered dragon tongue," I said. "What is it, really? A poison?"

"In a way, most certainly."

Which meant he'd just poisoned his own daughter.

He stood watching her from on high as she tried to spit out every last speck of what had been forced into her mouth. After a moment or two of this, he spoke.

"Tell us, Fah lo Suee: What was your plan?"

She clenched her jaw and clasped both hands over her mouth. Her face turned red as she held her breath, but finally her hands dropped to her sides and she began to speak.

"To use the dragon's tongue to make you discredit yourself before the Si-Fan council."

"For what purpose?"

"So that you would lose your position and I would ascend to it."

I noticed with a start that she'd lost her accent – her English was perfect.

"What's this mean?" I blurted. "What's happening?"

Her eyes blazed at me yet she answered calmly in an almost matter-of-fact tone. "The Si-Fan is a global organization that influences world events. My father holds high rank, but he has been diverting funds that should be flowing into the Si-Fan's coffers to a more personal concern: to fight the Japanese invaders in our homeland. I planned to slip some dragon tongue into his tea before the meeting so that he would admit his treachery himself."

I looked up at the Mandarin. "But you said it was poison."

He nodded. "The most dangerous poison of all: truth. One cannot deceive under influence of dragon's tongue."

I turned to her. "Why me?"

"Isn't it obvious, you oaf? You call yourself a detective? You went to Sorenson–"

"Ah, yes," the Mandarin said, raising a hand. "Detective Sorenson. He is no longer with us."

I groaned. "He thought he was going to make it."

"An error in judgment. One of many on the detective's part. But his travails helped pay for this cargo."

The daughter said, "He made errors, just as you made more than your share. You went to Sorenson, then went to Brannigan where you mentioned the jade container of dragon's tongue. I had been looking for a way to get my hands on that jar. You were perfect. Putty in my hands. So superior to the 'coolies,' the great white hero coming to the chinky-gal's rescue while using her for his own ends. After you opened the cabinet I was going to leave you to take the blame for the deaths of the staff and the attempted robbery."

"Attempted?"

"Of course. I needed less than a thimble's worth of the powder for my needs. My father wouldn't realize a little was missing. But his early return ruined everything."

She was right. I'd acted the fool and now I felt like one. All my years of experience and I let myself get played like a greenie. But I kept that hidden as I shook my head and stared at her

"What kind of daughter betrays her own father like that?"

My question must have triggered something because she launched into a tirade about how she'd never been allowed to see her mother, how she'd been ignored by a father whose life was filled with more important things than his daughter, who left her to be raised by a progression of strangers and then sent off to a succession of boarding schools. Betray her father? Why not? She hated him and would do a far better job for the Si-Fan than he.

By the end she'd collapsed to her knees in a sobbing heap.

I almost felt sorry for her, but self-pity never did anyone any good. And frankly, I'd trade her childhood for mine in a heartbeat.

"Do you have children, detective?" the Mandarin said.

"No."

"Why not?"

I looked up at those green eyes and realized he'd been watching me during his daughter's diatribe. Reading me like a book.

I couldn't hold his gaze. I looked away. "None of your beeswax."

He clapped his hands again. "Jiang Zhifu! Give our guest a taste of dragon's tongue."

My blood went icy and my gut crawled at the thought. I bit back a *No!* I didn't want to sound like the daughter, whatever her name was. I saw her grinning at me. She said nothing, but her eyes were full of anticipation.

Your turn!

No, not my turn. I'd never let this happen.

Spotting the powder on this guy Jiang Zhifu's fingertip as he approached, I took a boxer's stance. I was still feeling a little slow after being poisoned, but I could handle this coolie. He didn't slow his approach and I wasn't ready for his first move. Before he got within reach of my fists, his foot lashed out like a snake. I missed a block. He wore only soft slippers, but it felt like he'd driven the end of a two-by-four into my solar plexus. The air rushed out of me and wouldn't come back. As I keeled over onto my side, I felt his finger go into my mouth. I tried to bite it but it was gone before I could react. He wiped it on my shirt, then stepped back and stood with his hands behind him.

Three pairs of eyes watched me for a few minutes, then the Mandarin spoke.

"What is your name detective?"

I knew then he'd backgrounded me. When? When the Old Man had assigned me to find Margot Kachmar a couple of days ago? Or just yesterday when I'd contacted Sorenson? I tried my damnedest to give him the name on my gumshoe license, but it wouldn't come out. Because that wasn't the truth.

I couldn't hold back the words: "I don't know."

Then the questions began. Before long he'd filleted my life into twitching slivers. Everything I'd locked away from view – from everybody else's as well as my own – was paraded out for all to see: The nightmare string of foster homes where I'd been mistreated, each one progressively worse than the last. The beatings, the rapes by foster fathers and foster brothers, the humiliations, the helplessness, the deaf ears whenever I complained, the retaliations for complaining…everything was out there, all the feelings of worthlessness roared back as I relived those horrors.

By the end I was curled into the fetal position on the floor, sobbing harder than his daughter had a short while ago.

"Behold, Jiang Zhifu: one of those who look down on you, who dismiss you and call you names, who consider themselves lights of civilization in a world of barbarians and lesser beings. Trash! Treat him accordingly."

Jiang Zhifu bowed. "Yes, Illustrious."

I didn't – couldn't – resist as my hands were tied behind me. The collar was removed from my neck and I was dragged up to the deck. I could see the retreating glow of San Francisco lighting the fog across the water. We were at sea, a mile or two away.

"What are you going to do?" I said as I was shoved against the gunwale.

"As the Illustrious One ordered. Dispose of trash."

"Overboard? But I'll–!"

I almost said *drown*, but stopped myself. I'd already made a fool of myself. Of course I'd drown. Especially with my hands tied behind my back. That was the whole purpose.

I felt Jiang Zhifu's fingers working at the knots around my wrists. He freed them.

"What–?"

"You have terrible life. You will die in water, but not without chance."

I realized this was no small gesture. He was going against his master. I looked at him but could read nothing in those black eyes.

Before I could thank him he pushed me.

I tumbled over the gunwale but managed to straighten my body so I hit feet first. The icy water closed over me. I shuddered and fought my way to the surface, gasping for air as the freighter lumbered on. I wasted no time. I kicked off my shoes and began stroking toward the glow of the city.

The frightened little-boy part of my brain the dragon tongue had awakened whined that I had no chance. If the cold didn't seize up my muscles, I'd run out of gas before I made the dock.

I didn't listen. His incessant whining was why I'd locked him away years ago. Sure my chances were slim. Less than slim. But I was going to make it. And then I was going to devote my life to tracking down the Mandarin or the Lord of Strange Deaths or whoever he really was. No doubt he already had a slew of people on his trail. Well, now he had one more.

Trash? We'd see about that.

The Teen Trilogy
Jack: Secret Histories
Jack: Secret Circles
Jack: Secret Vengeance

The Early Years Trilogy
Cold City
Dark City
Fear City

The LaNague Federation Series
Healer
Wheels Within Wheels
An Enemy of the State
Dydeetown World
The Tery

Other Novels
Black Wind
Sibs
The Select
Virgin
Implant
Deep as the Marrow
Mirage (with Matthew J. Costello)
Nightkill (with Steven Spruill)
DNA Wars (formerly *Masque* with M. J. Costello)
Sims
The Fifth Harmonic
Midnight Mass
The Proteus Cure (with Tracy L. Carbone)
A Necessary End (with Sarah Pinborough)
Panacea

The Nocturnia Chronicles (with Tom
Monteleone)
Definitely Not Kansas
Family Secrets
The Silent Ones

Short Fiction
Soft & Others
The Barrens & Others
The Christmas Thingy
Aftershock & Others
*The Peabody-Ozymandias Traveling Circus &
Oddity Emporium*
Quick Fixes – Tales of Repairman Jack
Sex Slaves of the Dragon Tong

Editor
Freak Show
Diagnosis: Terminal
The Hogben Chronicles (with Pierce Watters)

Omnibus Editions
The Complete LaNague
Calling Dr. Death (3 medical thrillers)

Made in the USA
Lexington, KY
06 November 2017